Gambling on Her Dragon

Book 1
Shifters in Vegas

von Anna Lowe

Contents

Free Books

Get your free e-books now!

Sign up for my newsletter at *annalowebooks.com* to get three free books!

- *Desert Wolf*: Friend or Foe (Book 1.1 in the Twin Moon Ranch series)

- *Off the Charts* (the prequel to the Serendipity Adventure series)

- *Perfection* (the prequel to the Blue Moon Saloon series)

Chapter One

Trey groaned and flexed his fingers, wondering where he was. He cracked an eye open and immediately let it slide shut.

Damn, did his head hurt. Which didn't make sense because the rest of his body felt strangely satisfied. Warm, honey-in-the-veins satisfied, like he'd come straight from a hot tub and not a fogbank of blurry memories of the night before.

He really ought to force his eyes open and look around, but something told him reality wouldn't be too good. Better to go back to that dream — the one with the redhead clawing his back and moaning his name. That was sure to be better than whatever reality he would eventually have to wake up to.

Because, shit. He didn't even know which town or city he was in.

Vegas, his inner wolf hummed. *Nighttime. Not a full moon, so shut up and get back to sleep.*

Vegas. That part, he remembered. But the rest... The rest was kind of fuzzy. The hum of a crowd, the electric ping of slot machines, the smacking shuffle of cards. The quiet *chink* of casino chips — a big stack of them, piled high by his left hand. And beyond that, a pair of lagoon-green eyes like none he'd ever seen. Like sea glass, glinting in the morning light.

His wolf let out a dreamy sigh, and his pulse quickened just a bit.

Christ, how much had he been drinking? What had he been up to last night?

He slid a hand under the sheets — crisp, white hotel sheets — and found something warm. Warm and soft on the surface, but nicely tight underneath. Something that begged to be stroked... Admired... Maybe even kissed.

1

He snuggled a little closer and kept his eyes firmly shut, because his brain was most definitely not ready for visuals yet. His head was still throbbing, his memories a jigsaw puzzle.

Green eyes. Auburn hair. A mouth that was pure sin. He remembered that much, but the features refused to come together and came out like one of those mismatched Picasso faces instead.

His hand slid over a curve and arrived at something even softer, and a happy little coo sounded in return.

A woman.

Huh.

A headache *and* a woman. In Vegas. Why was he not surprised?

While the human part of his mind scrambled for an explanation, his inner wolf yawned and made him tug her closer. *Mine. All mine.*

His human side groaned, but his wolf let out a rumble of satisfaction that traveled all the way through his body and back again.

The wires in his brain crossed and instead of rolling away, he nestled closer. Nice and cozy, so he could inhale her lavender scent. He wrapped his hand the rest of the way over the glorious swell of a breast, resting his elbow in the perfect nook of her waist. The woman arched into his chest and purred, and his cock twitched.

Really, his brain should have gone on red alert right there. But the only part of his body that seemed to respond was his cock, and that, in double time. He pulled her closer — and closer still when she pushed her perfect curve of an ass into his groin.

She rolled toward him, inviting his head to follow his hand to her chest. Familiar territory, somehow, because his lips found their way right to the world's tightest, tastiest nipple and licked.

"Mmm," she hummed, stroking his back.

His brain was still back at the starting blocks. *Whoa, what the—*

Don't overthink, his wolf growled. *Just enjoy. Partake. Feast.*

He was in human form, but the wolf was firmly in charge, because damn, did he feast. He suckled that sweet bud, kneaded the soft flesh, and growled with lust at the sounds coming from her.

"Trey... God, yes. Don't stop... "

He wracked his muddled mind for her name, but he kept coming up with a blank. Shit. Cindy? Laura? Tara?

His body sure seemed to know hers, though, because their legs didn't tangle so much as mesh. He recognized the peach-cream scent of her skin and the tight checkerboard of her hard abs. The lift of her mound, and the glorious plunge to heaven, hidden between her legs.

Legs she wrapped around him, drawing him in.

His fingers slid south from her belly button like they'd traveled that delicious path a hundred times before.

"Trey," she panted.

Good thing his wolf filled in with a lusty growl, because he had no clue what to say... No clue why his entire body was on fire for her instead of just his dick... And definitely no clue why this moment felt like a major milestone and not just another roll in the hay.

Damn. Maybe he hadn't just been drinking, but smoking some weird shit, too, because his soul was sobbing and singing hallelujah at the same time. The messed-up, joyful sob of a man who'd found something he thought he'd lost forever.

Which was weird, because Trey hadn't lost anything. He hadn't been looking for anything, either — nothing other than a six-week road trip and a bit of fun before settling down to a new job back on the East Coast.

Man, that truck driver he'd hitched a ride into Vegas with was right. *You gotta be careful in Vegas, son...*

His eyes finally joined the party, and the sight of the woman knocked his breath away. Glossy auburn hair splayed over the pillow, shining so brightly, she seemed to glow. A row of perfect ivory teeth flashed in a blissed-out smile. High, Audrey Hepburn cheekbones cast shadows over her face, forming a landscape of their own. Her lips opened and closed and sighed as she breathed his name.

Her eyes slid open, and he lost his breath again. Like she'd just shoved aside a sky full of clouds and let summer shine down, filling everything with happiness and light.

So, yeah, he must have smoked some weird shit last night. But God, he'd go with the flow right now, because nothing had ever made him feel quite this good. The only one of his senses that wasn't completely on fire was his strangely muted sense of smell, which still appeared to be asleep. Not that he needed his nose to enjoy *this*.

"Trey..." she murmured, pulling him closer.

It was like one of those crazy Greek myths he'd read about in fifth grade where a goddess would come down to Earth to screw a hapless shepherd who'd caught her eye and eventually set off a whole series of unforeseen events — such as pissing off her immortal god husband who would summon storms, flood rivers, and permanently skew the seasons to obliterate the poor sap caught balls deep in heaven. A god who would change the world forever, all in the name of revenge.

Trey tried to shake the crazy feeling away, but one part stuck. The part about the world changing forever. His world, at least.

He let his body slide over hers, hoping to hell there was no pissed off god standing by with a couple of lightning bolts.

"Trey..."

The muscles of her chiseled swimmer's shoulders flexed, and she extended her arms overhead, lifting her breasts. He plunged in, and even in the searing heat that blurred his vision for the next few seconds, his hands found hers instinctively. Their fingers interlaced as he pushed forward, burying himself deep.

"Kaya..." He moaned at the fireworks rocketing inside, then allowed himself a ridiculously proud grin. He knew her name, which meant he wasn't a total prick. Just a messed-up guy wondering how he'd found heaven in a city that seemed a lot closer to hell.

"Deeper," she urged him. "Faster."

They started pumping in perfect rhythm, both of them, with him sliding forward and her bucking to meet him, sighing a little each time. God, she was tight. Perfect. And buff, because she greeted every hot, hard slide with a firm squeeze of rippling muscle as he plunged deeper, deeper — Christ, so deep — with her milking him all the way.

"Kaya. . ."

Now he was the one crying her name. But then again, a guy couldn't be expected to keep his cool with a goddess, right?

A goddess who rocked her head from side to side and cried out. Her six-pack stomach rippled — yeah, he looked, because how could he not? — and he could feel her tight grip on him inside. He drank in the sight of her face, twisted in ecstasy.

His wolf growled as he kissed the hollow of her neck, where her pulse danced under his tongue.

Now. We take her now!

His canines pushed through his gums and scraped along her skin.

"Yes. . ." she whispered.

He couldn't see any more. He couldn't hear. Everything boiled down to the raging heat in his body and the overwhelming need to claim.

Take her! Make her ours!

What should have sounded crazy sounded just right. Making her his. . . Sealing the future, right there and then. He could keep this goddess forever and—

Every alarm in his body started clanging, including one that sounded like a submarine, ready to dive deep. *A-woo-ga! A-woo-ga!*

He wrestled his wolf back into its inner cage and threw his full weight against the door. Mentally, at least. Physically, his body was still pumping hard, hurtling them both toward release.

But, damn. What the hell was the beast thinking, nipping at her neck?

Make her our mate. His wolf rattled the bars of its cage, looking for a weak spot.

No biting, he snarled back. *No claiming.*

She wants us! the wolf fought protested. *Look at her!*

She moaned and pulled her legs higher around his waist, making his eyes roll back in his head.

Mate, mate, mate. His body took up the chant in time to the wild beat of his heart.

He shook his head. He might be dumb enough to get drunk in Vegas. He might be bold enough to take a girl he didn't know to a hotel room. He might be crazy enough to think they were good together. But he wasn't completely nuts. He didn't want or need a mate. Hell, he didn't even believe in destined mates.

Not even when she's wrapped around you, screaming your name?

He shut out the wolf and concentrated on the tight ache of his body. His last, hard thrust had him exploding deep inside her. All he registered was the heady sensation of free-falling over a glorious mountain cliff.

He panted into her skin... Hid his face in the sheets... Wondered when the lightning bolt would strike him down. He counted the beats of her heart, slowing down in perfect time with his, and he stroked her silky hair, breathing her in.

Slowly, Kaya went from throes-of-passion tension to a loose snuggle, and brushed the length of his right eyebrow with her finger in wordless wonder.

When she slid her eyes shut, it scared the hell out of him. What if that was regret? Rejection? A precursor to good-bye?

He held her a little tighter, just in case.

She twisted gently in his arms, not quite making an escape, not quite letting down her guard. Just settling into a spooned position, exactly how that crazy night started out.

Except it hadn't started there. Trey racked his brain, trying to remember something. Anything.

But he couldn't quite focus on anything because the feel of her in his arms affected him like a drug, and he drifted off again in spite of the thousand questions rocking his hazy mind.

Chapter Two

Trey dreamed of roulette wheels and spitting slot machines. Flying aces and bleeding hearts and the king of spades...

He woke with a jolt, reaching for Kaya in the dark.

He reached a little farther, but she wasn't there.

The sheets were still warm, though, so she couldn't be far. But where did she go?

The curtains flapped in a weak desert breeze, and he rolled toward the balcony. He sighed deeply at the sight of Kaya leaning against the rail, looking up at the stars. At least, whatever stars were visible in the lights of a city that didn't recognize the boundary between day and night.

She was an ivory statue against the night sky, chiseled by a master artist who liked his models sinewy, tall, and strong. Feminine at the same time, though, thanks to the light curves and the way she tilted her hips.

Hips he'd recently had squeezed against his in a horizontal samba of the very best kind.

Torn between admiring the goddess and calling the mystery woman back to his side, he just watched her. Who was she? What was she doing in Vegas? Where was she going next?

His mind spun off on a thousand fantasies. Maybe she was road-tripping, too. Heading west, like him, on her very first trip to the Pacific coast. Maybe they could travel together. Maybe he could learn more about her than the sleek lines of her body and the sharp shudder of her breath when he moved inside her. A lot more, even, than the way she caught her lower lip in her teeth or the way her eyes made his insides sing. Maybe—

Something scratched at the door, and he sat up with a jolt, straining his ears.

"Shh. Pick the lock," someone whispered outside.

"Step back," a deep voice replied. The kind of deep voice that belonged to a big, bad bouncer-type.

A human might have slept right through that, but his wolf ears caught every word.

"Two minutes from now, that wad of cash is ours."

Trey's ears twitched. Wad of cash? What cash?

"Yeah," the second voice replied. "And the bounty, too."

He glanced at the woman, who was tense now, coiled like a spring.

A memory came hurtling out of nowhere and smacked him on the back of his head. Cards... Poker... Chips... Lots and lots of chips, standing in uneven piles. Two hands reaching out and scooping the piles toward his chest. *His* hands, because there was the little scar on the knuckles on the right.

Apparently, he'd gotten lucky in more than one way last night. With cards *and* with a girl.

His gut lurched as he blinked back to reality and studied Kaya. What if the money was the only thing that had drawn her to him?

Don't be ridiculous, his wolf huffed. *She's not the type.*

He frowned. As if the beast could judge her character on the basis of a couple of hot, hard fucks.

Heavenly fucks, the wolf corrected him. *And believe me, our mate isn't the type.*

Right. She'd jumped in the sack with a stranger. What type did that make her?

An itch formed on the back of his neck. What type did that make him?

They stood staring at each other, eyes shining in the darkness.

Then the doorknob rattled again, and the man outside swore.

Kaya whirled, and Trey jerked his head toward her again. What had she been looking for, leaning over the balcony rail like that?

Some way to escape, dumbass, a distant part of his mind registered.

He sprang out of bed and stretched to his full height. His considerable height, thank goodness, because what was about to come through the door was plenty big, too.

His nostrils flared, catching a musky, cave scent. Crap. The two thugs outside were bear shifters.

Something scraped on the balcony, and he glanced back. It was like a goddamn tennis match, with the door on his right and the balcony on his left. On the balcony, Kaya grabbed a canvas bag that looked awfully familiar as she pulled a chair up to the railing.

The railing she climbed up on.

Every nerve in his body screamed. *Holy shit!*

He rushed toward her. "Don't jump!"

He had no clue what floor they were on, but even a beat-up, outdated hotel like this had to be high enough to kill.

Kaya, however, just leaned farther over the edge.

"Stop!" He wrestled past the curtains and tripped over the track of the sliding door.

Kaya teetered on the rail, eyeing the fall.

"Don't!" He scrambled to his feet, reaching out.

She might have said something, but he couldn't hear anything but the pounding of his heart.

Everything slurred into slow motion. Kaya's toes curled over the rail, right at his eye level. Her arms swept wide, and the bag dangled under one of them. Her hair played in the wind as if she were at a lakeside and not several stories up. Six stories, minimum, he decided, eyeing the space beyond the rails. No pool waiting to catch his lover, either — just a dirty back lot.

His hamstrings screamed as he hurtled upward. His bare feet were cold on the tile floor. He stretched desperately, reaching past her fingers to grab at her wrist.

The scent of open desert reached his nostrils, mocking his effort to cheat death.

Kaya bent her knees, then straightened, and her feet left the rail. She was airborne.

Her fingers slipped past his. For one glorious, hope-filled instant, his hand was warm. The next, it was empty, and his heart slammed against his ribs.

He crashed into the cold metal of the wrought iron railing and heaved halfway out, still reaching.

"No!" he screamed from the bottom of his soul, like she wasn't a perfect stranger but his closest, oldest friend.

His own cry echoed in his ears as he watched her hurtle to certain death.

She didn't fall the way people in movies fell, though. Not stone-stiff, like she was already dead. Not clawing at the air, searching for some ephemeral grip. Not screeching or flailing one bit.

Nope. She dove. The most graceful swan dive he'd ever seen. Arms wide, legs straight, body curved. So perfect, he nearly double-checked to see if there was a pool down there, after all.

Then her arms spread wider, and he blinked, because it looked a lot more like a skydiver's controlled free fall than a deathly drop. More like a glide, actually, with shoulders so broad they might have been extending to wings. Feet so tight, they might have been a tail.

He gripped the railing tighter and stared. Shadows dappled over her body until he thought he was seeing things. Her arms looked unnaturally wide. Her fingers so long, he could make out each one.

Kaya?

He blinked as his death-bound lover swooped upward in a long, graceful arc. Her skin became tough and leathery, and her arms stretched into wings. Her tail snapped like a whip, her wings beat, and she shot up like an arrow.

Trey gaped as the truth slowly registered. His mystery lover was a dragon shifter. A beautiful, petite dragon with scales tinted reddish-black.

He brought his hand to his nose and sniffed, testing her scent. The shifter part was faint and heavily layered with the fragrance of sex and desire. Whatever weird drug he'd been under the influence of must have intoxicated his nose most of all, if he hadn't picked up the shifter part until now.

And now was too late.

She swung her neck north, and the long body followed with an effortless beat of the wings. Her tail arced, her body rippled, and she flew out of sight behind a towering high-rise. She shot out the other side, then rose against the orb of the nearly full moon with that bag clutched in her claw.

Trey clung to the railing hard so hard, he might as well have been swinging on the wrong side. He strained his eyes, but the night sky had already secreted Kaya away. A second later, he slumped to his ass on the balcony.

Lover...dragon...

Dragon with a bag...

Wait a minute. His bag? The bag he'd put his money in?

He groaned and held his head in his hands. For all of two seconds, until the door to the room crashed open and two figures burst inside. Human except for their fangs.

The one on the left crouched into a wary attack pose. The one on the right grinned and strode forward with a cocky step.

"Wolf," the thug growled, slamming a fist into his own hand in a warm-up blow, "you're going to regret ever coming to Vegas."

Trey nearly snorted. Regret coming to Vegas? He already did.

.

Chapter Three

Kaya flew in a tight loop, trying to clear her head. She dipped a wing, dropped into a barrel roll, and then climbed straight toward the moon. No matter what she tried, though, she still tingled all over — and not from shifting.

Damn it! She was still tingling from *him*. Which was really, really not what she'd had planned for the night.

But, crap. Nothing had gone as planned. All she'd been after was a quick eighty thousand dollars. Sex had never been part of the plan. It was supposed to be a quick in-and-out job—

She stopped the thought there with a grimace. Bad word choice, because somehow she'd let the night turn into an entirely different kind of in-and-out. Not her going in and eventually coming out of the casino, thousands richer than she'd started. No — it had been Trey, sliding in and out of her body. Gripping her hands like he never wanted to let go. Not just exploring her body, but worshiping it. Looking into her eyes as if he was just as transfixed as she by whatever magic had sprung up between the two of them that night.

She dove into another roll and used the chance to fan her face with her left wing, because just thinking about Cowboy Scrumptious had her overheating again.

Not just a man. A wolf, the little voice at the back of her mind reminded her.

A wolf shifter who looked just like the mystery man who starred in her lustiest fantasies. She'd always thought that face was a figment of her imagination, but now, she wasn't so sure.

She'd watched him from the moment he walked into the casino, because how could she *not* watch a man like that? A

13

ANNA LOWE

man who prowled more than he walked, like a lion on the
savannah or a boxer stepping into a ring. A man whose aura
reached out in front of him like a couple of body guards yelling,
Clear the way! Clear the way!

Not that he needed bodyguards, not with a build like that.
People had unconsciously ducked away from those broad shoulders and powerful legs as if clearing space for a herd of bulls.

A man with patience, brains, and an endearing touch of
innocence. He'd circled the poker tables a couple of times —
watching, waiting, quietly observing. When he finally decided
on one, he slid into an empty chair like a bull rider climbing
into the starting pen. Wary. Confident. Ready for the ride of
his life. Impossibly blue — peacock blue — eyes had studied
the deck as if he had X-ray vision and could guess what was
coming next. Not that he'd been counting cards or pulling any
of the usual tricks, because he simply glanced once at his cards,
made up his mind, and sat back to wait.

Gimme what you got, fate. That's what his body language
had said.

Not, *Watch out, sucker, I've got an ace up my sleeve.*

Just about the only trick he'd pulled was when he glanced
up and met her gaze. *Captured* her gaze was more like it, even
from twenty feet away, because she couldn't drag it away after
that. And hell, he couldn't seem to, either. His bottom lip had
swung open as if he'd never seen anything like her before.

And she hadn't even been in her dragon form.

She'd been just Kaya. Kaya, the veterinarian's assistant,
with straight hair, small boobs, and a tendency to frown when
she was thinking.

She rode an updraft on wide, steady wings, trying to rein
in her racing pulse.

So, big deal. She'd seen a good-looking man. A good-
looking man with just enough of a lucky streak to become her
target that night.

But it wasn't that simple, because she hadn't been the only
one watching him. The two bounty hunters had zeroed right in
on him, too. She'd seen them in action when frequenting the
casino over the past couple of days. The big one had brushed

14

right past her, reeking of bear. Not the pure, woodsy scent she'd caught coming off the handsome wolf shifter, but the pungent smell of a dank and dirty winter cave.

She'd seen the two thugs shift their focus from a scrawnier guy to him. Dollar signs practically lit up in their eyes like spinning symbols in slot machines. They recruited for the fighting pits, and a wolf like Trey was the perfect candidate. He would fight long and hard. He might even survive in the fight pits for a couple of weeks, bringing thousands to the bookies the thugs had partnered with.

The fighting pits were Vegas' best-kept secret. Or one of Vegas' many secrets, anyway. An arena in which bets weren't won and lost with cards but with lives. Animal lives, shifter lives. The colosseums of ancient Rome had nothing on the fight pits, judging by what she'd caught from whispers and hushed tones.

The big bounty hunter had muscled past her and taken up position on the right side of the table, watching Trey take his cards. After a while, the man sniffed and nodded.

Kaya had followed the bounty hunter's gaze to the opposite end of the table. Who was he signaling to?

Probably not the anorexic doe shifter with big hair and fake boobs. She was too busy hanging over her sugar daddy, a balding human. Not the down-and-out werebear, lumbering toward the slot machines, nor the unicorn shifter who pranced by in a tuxedo that was a little too tight in the ass.

No, the thug had nodded to a second bear shifter. A skinnier one in the brown suit that all the employees wore. He nodded back, disappeared, and came back two minutes later with a tray full of drinks. She'd bet her life that one of them was spiked.

"Whiskey, sir?"

Hot Stuff nodded absently as he turned two cards in for two new ones, not noticing a thing. Within a couple of rounds, he'd drained the glass.

Jesus. Hadn't anyone warned this cowboy about Vegas? Whatever poker he'd learned must have been in a bunkhouse out on some ranch and not in a two-faced place like a casino that played by its own rules.

The drug would take a while to work on his shifter metabolism, but it would kick in eventually. The thugs would wait until he could no longer see straight, then make their move, and he would wake up in a dungeon five stories underground, ready to be cast into the pits.

How could he be so naive?

But she'd been no better, drowning in the universe of blue in his eyes. Like she'd been drugged, too. Drugged on his eyes, his scent, his soft touch. Oh, Lord, what had she done?

She huffed her frustration into the night, and — *whoa!*

A thin trickle of fire exploded from her mouth.

Holy shit.

She lost her rhythm momentarily and had to shake out her wings before she got them to flap in sync again. The fire had gone out of her dragon clan generations ago. Nowadays, only the mightiest could summon up a good, old-fashioned, barn-burning inferno. The best Kaya had ever managed was little coughing flames that snuffed out almost before they started. Baby flames that tasted like ash and smelled of rotten egg — and that, only when she was really worked up.

Her grandfather had been full of stories of old dragon ways. *Fire isn't kindled by greed or desire,* she remembered him explaining as they flew side by side, years ago. *Fire is kindled by love, and if you truly believe. . .*

She snorted. Sure. Love. She barely knew the man she'd slept with.

The ridiculously attractive man with a voice that tickled something deep in her soul.

She flew toward the purplish-brown mountains in the distance, wondering why she was so worked up.

It was her sister. That's what it was — anxiety for her sister, because it sure as hell couldn't be the man. Definitely, definitely not the man.

She banked around a bend in the first valley and dropped into a canyon. With one strong flap of her wings, she rose and wheeled to land on a ledge on the south side. That ledge was where she had set up a lair for the duration of her stay in Vegas, while she figured out what to do about her sister.

Having the bag clutched between her claws meant she had to land one-footed, and she shifted so fast that when she came to a halt, it was on human feet. She rolled her shoulders as the farthest edge of her wings retreated beneath her skin. Then she cracked her neck a little, left then right. Flexing her fingers a couple of times, she closed her eyes, getting used to the sensation of breathing down a shorter windpipe again.

Dawn was just breaking over the desert, and it was beautiful. Faint yellow-and-pink light filtered over the hills, working its way deeper into the valleys, inch by scrubby inch. An owl hooted somewhere over to the left, saying goodbye to the night.

A beautiful day. So why was her stomach tied into knots?

She sat on a rock, dumped out the contents of the bag, and started counting and recounting the bills.

"Eighty-seven thousand... eighty-eight thousand..." She counted out loud, telling herself it was real. She had enough. More than enough, as it turned out. Ninety thousand, altogether.

She gave a little fist pump and slid a hand into her back pocket, but it just bumped off her bare flesh.

Her breath caught, and the little high of triumph still coursing through her veins turned to ice.

Her clothes. Her jeans. Her phone...

She'd left them all behind in the hotel room.

Her blood slowed in her veins. She hadn't been that careless, had she?

Oh, God. Yes, she had. She'd only brought the money bag out to the balcony for a quick count while Trey was asleep. She'd planned — Truly! Honestly! — to take only what she needed and leave him the rest. There was no way she could have guessed that the thugs would show up just then and rouse Trey out of bed.

Trey, in all his naked glory. Trey, blinking the sleep out of his eyes.

Trey's eyes going wide as he saw her getting ready to jump.

Her heart thumped, replaying it all.

He'd leaped for her, stretching like an Olympic athlete, reaching with all his might. Yelling in fear, like she'd never heard a man yell before. Not for himself, but for her.

And what had she done?

Kaya let her eyes slide shut in shame. She'd grabbed the money and flown the coop. Literally.

For all that she tried gulping away the lump in her throat, it stayed stubbornly stuck.

She shook her head and gave herself a stern lecture. The only thing that mattered was the money for her sister. Trey would have given her the money if she'd had a chance to explain why she needed it so badly, right? Especially if she had explained why he was her only hope.

When she cleared her throat, the ashy taste of fire was still there. Trey had won those thousands easily. He could win another couple of thousand just as easily, right?

She had to get Hot Stuff out of her mind. She had to move on, because the last thing she needed was a card-playing wolf in her life. What she needed was to concentrate and get on with her plan.

A plan which called for her phone, an unlisted number, and a wad of cash.

And crap, she was one for three, because the phone and the number were back in the hotel room, along with her clothes.

She sat down on the rock so hard, it hurt. But hell, she deserved it for being that dumb.

Tears welled up but she blinked them away because that wouldn't help. What she needed was a plan. A new plan.

She groaned and hung her head in her hands.

A plan that meant she wasn't through with Hot Stuff, after all.

Chapter Four

Trey looked left and right then hustled out the back door. Out in the alley, the temperature soared to a skin-scorching hundred-plus degrees, even in the morning shade. He shouldered his backpack and checked the watch he'd just had time to grab after bouncing the two thugs off the wall in the hotel room and racing out the door.

Seven a.m.

Man, oh man, it was going to be a hell of a day — following a hell of a night. How did an innocent detour to Vegas turn into... into... this hornet's nest he'd gotten himself tangled up in?

He put his hat on — his lucky hat, a going-away present from his cousin Lana — and took off down the alley. Once he rounded the corner to Fremont Street, he jumped in the first available cab.

"Where to, buddy?" The driver glanced at him in the rearview mirror. Once, not twice, which was good. No need for anyone to remember him, just in case.

His mind spun. Where to? What he really needed to do was get the hell out of town. Pronto.

But before he could stop it, his wolf made him say something totally different. "A good breakfast place on the far side of town."

The driver flashed a crooked smile. "Lemme guess. Fun night with a pretty girl turns into a quick exit?"

Trey sighed and flopped back against the seat. If only the guy knew how quick an exit it had been. The last hit of adrenaline was still washing through his veins, rapidly turning to a weary throb. He could still feel the brush of Kaya's fingers against his, the backwash of her wings...

Her *wings*, dammit!

It wasn't that he didn't know dragons existed. But he'd never, ever seen one, much less slept with one, or woken up to a fist-fight over one. His knuckles throbbed from the punch he'd thrown at one thug's temple, and his shoulder still felt the lead weight of the second guy he'd body checked into the wall. The headache was back, too, along with the questions.

Who was dragon lady? Where did she go? Would he ever see her again?

He cleared his throat, because that last part sounded a little too close to a whimper, even in his mind.

"Welcome to Las Vegas, man," the cab driver chuckled. "I know just the place for a morning-after breakfast. Best coffee in town."

The coffee was mud, as it turned out, and Trey wasn't sure who that said more about — the cab driver's judgment or the quality of Vegas' coffee. But the omelet was good, and he'd succeeded in leaving a cold trail the bear shifters couldn't follow. He had a separate stash of money to pay for the cab and breakfast, but it sure wasn't what he'd had in that canvas bag Kaya had flown off with.

He scraped the last bit of sticky yolk off his plate with his toast and considered his next move. And he nearly choked on the next slurp of coffee when his wolf chimed in with its two cents.

Find Kaya. Hold her. Hug her. Make her our mate.

He slammed the coffee cup down so hard, three heads turned his way. What had gotten into his beast?

Destiny, the wolf purred, driving an image of the woman into his mind. A very dangerous image of open lips, hungry eyes, and flaring nostrils, as if the same magnetic force that had moved him had acted on her, too.

Mate, the wolf concluded. *Mine.*

He shook his head the way he always had at that destined mate nonsense. Just because the occasional shifter fell head over heels in love with another didn't mean it was destiny at work.

But then another image of Kaya jumped out of his garbled memories and socked him in the gut. The moment he'd lifted his eyes from another winning hand of cards — royal flush, no less, his second of the night — and saw her, he'd stopped breathing and sipping the whiskey in his right hand. He'd quit fingering the five-thousand-dollar chip in his left hand, because time had screeched to a fender-crushing halt and flopped over dead in its tracks, right there and then.

Her eyes were wider and brighter than the Nevada sky. The Arizona sky, too — all of it. She stared back in wonder and excitement, as if time had stood still for her, too. Then his mind had fast-forwarded into a jumpy reel of footage of all the wonders the future might hold if only the two of them grabbed hold of this moment and hung on with all their might. It was the chance of their lives, and it was fluttering by like a winning lottery ticket pushed by hurricane-force winds. Every cell, every atom in his body screamed at him to reach out and grab before his big chance got away.

He'd gotten so lost in those eyes, he nearly missed his chance to lay down his cards before the dealer called the round. By some miracle, he'd tossed his hand down just in time, along with the five-thousand-dollar chip, and he didn't even soak in the cheer of amazement that went up all around. All he saw was her.

Kaya. Goddess. Dragon lady. Destined mate?

Or Kaya, playgirl and thief?

He let out a long, wavering breath, because the memories slowly filtering back into his consciousness all pranced around the same five-figure sum. Ninety thousand dollars. He'd won ninety thousand! That part hadn't been a dream, just like meeting Kaya hadn't been a dream.

A phone rang, and he shot slitty looks around the nearby tables because it sure wasn't his. He sipped his coffee, annoyed.

You gonna get that, buddy? the guy in the next booth asked with a sharp look.

Trey glared back until he realized the sound was coming from his backpack. Then he grabbed it from under the table and rooted around inside. On his escape from the hotel room, he'd just managed to snatch the bag and an armful of clothes. He'd pulled on his jeans and shirt in the stairwell once he was sure he had a decent lead on the thugs, but the rest he'd stuffed into the bag before hurrying on.

He opened it now, keeping it low and out of sight of the dull-eyed diner patrons, some of whom stared off into their own memories, others into regrets.

Kaya's scent filtered out before he could reach into the backpack, making his pulse skip. Then his fingers closed around something small and hard, and he pulled out the phone and stared at it through another two rings. Finally, he hit *receive* and grunted a neutral greeting.

"Do you have the money?" someone barked.

He considered that one for a moment. How the hell to answer, if he should answer at all? Kaya had the money, all right. But maybe that wasn't the best answer.

"Soon." A neutral enough reply, he figured.

"Soon? Soon?" The voice rose in anger. "You know what I'll do if you don't bring me the money?"

A muffled bang came through the phone, and a woman yelped in pain. "Oh my God, Kaya. I'm so sorry!"

The phone jerked back to the heavy-breathing man.

"Message clear? I want my money."

Jesus, what was going on?

Trey's mind raced. It was time to bluff. "I'll add five to the deal."

The voice scoffed but Trey waited. He had no idea what he was promising or to whom. Five hundred dollars? Five thousand? Five million? But he had to do something.

"Ten," the shadowy voice demanded.

And just like that, he had a deal. A deal he had no idea whether he could uphold.

"Soon." He nodded into the phone.

"Midnight," the man hissed.

And, *bang!* Call over.

He stared at the phone. What the hell was going on?

It occurred to him that maybe the bag held another clue, so he dug in. Carefully, for some reason, as if his great-grandma's china might be in there. The top item was Kaya's shirt. A sheer, silky thing almost as nice to touch as her hair. Without thinking, he held it up to his nose for a deep sniff, then shoved it back into his lap and glanced around.

Everyone's eyes were on the keno screen. Whew. If he wasn't careful, he'd be sniffing her panties in broad daylight next.

Which wasn't the point. Not that he knew exactly what the point was, but he kept picking through her clothes anyway.

Pants. One shoe. A black, lacy bra that made his cock itch. A pretty polka dot scarf...

His hand hit the bottom of the backpack. No cash. No canvas stash bag he'd stuffed his winnings in before leaving the casino and heading out with Kaya on his arm. She'd taken him on all kinds of wild detours on the way to the hotel room, and his vision had blurred with every step. Everything had blurred but her.

Kaya on his arm... He replayed that moment, again and again. She'd hooked her elbow through his and kissed his ear even before they got to the room.

He rummaged some more until he was sure. His wallet was still in there with the couple of hundred bucks he'd entered Vegas with, but nothing else. No wads of cash.

No dragon lady.

Which made her a thief, right?

Trey took another sip of muddy coffee while his wolf let out a long, mournful howl.

The two thugs sure hadn't gotten ahold of anything. He'd been too quick for that. He hadn't left his winnings back in the room. And Kaya had flown off with a bag in her claws.

So, yeah, dragon lady was a thief, all right.

He tried to be furious. Truly, he did, working really, really hard to muster up some bitterness or rage. Ninety thousand dollars! Ninety grand! Enough to buy him the kind of property he dreamed of. Something small, up in the mountains, where the air was cleaner, the creek water cooler, the stars closer at night. Kaya had stolen all that from him, so he had every right to hate those gorgeous eyes, those alluring curves.

All he managed to work up, though, was the beginning of another hard-on, just from picturing her.

With a few finger taps, he checked her outgoing calls and her contacts list. Then he rummaged in her pant pockets, telling himself it was to find some clue to her identity and not to get off on the thought of sliding his hands in there when she still had them on, as he was pretty sure he'd done before stripping her naked last night. Which would have happened about five seconds after she'd stripped him, if shaky memory served.

Had all that been an act, or had she needed him the way he needed her? The crazy hunger, the sheer, animal urge. Had she felt it, too?

Thoughts like those got him nowhere, other than the full-on boner now testing the seams of his jeans.

One of her pant pockets held a couple of scraps that didn't tell him anything much. A receipt for snacks at a gas station, a couple of scratched keno cards, and the sum total of seven bucks, folded into eighths. The other pocket held a business card — *Igor Schiller, Scarlet Palace* — with a mobile number penciled onto the back, plus a slip of paper he held up to the light.

Graceland Valet Parking, it read, with a number, time, and date. Three days ago.

He looked at the business card then at the parking slip. Where to start?

He stuck the business card in his own pocket and kept the parking slip out. Kaya had his cash, so it would only be fair to start with her car, right?

"Where to?" the next cab driver he found asked.

He flashed the stub, and the driver took off, crooning an Elvis song.

Trey held out the ticket stub, trying not to squint at the white sequined suit flashing at him like a thousand fragments of the pounding desert sun.

The Elvis impersonator whistled. "Three days, mister. Gonna be a hell of a bill."

A jaunty tune bounced out of the speakers overhead. Another Presley tune, of course.

Trey shrugged. "Can you just get the car, please?"

"Sweet ride." Elvis grinned, making his sideburns bend. "Gonna hate to see her go."

Trey forked over the three-figure fee without so much as a whimper, which was nuts. He'd been stretching every one of his hard-earned dollars as far as he could, but somehow, this seemed worth the splurge. Anything associated with Kaya was worth the splurge.

He craned his neck as the guy strode down the rows of cars and disappeared around the back. A BMW with Oregon plates caught his eye on the right, and a Lexus with tinted windows on the left. Somewhere farther down the line, the Thule rack atop an SUV stood out, carrying two mud-splattered mountain bikes. No real dingers here — they were all pretty nice rides.

What would Kaya drive? A convertible Beetle, like the powder-blue one parked on the right? A sensible Prius, like the one in the second row?

Static scratched from the speakers of Graceland Parking before another lovestruck Elvis tune poured out, featuring shaky knees, stuttering words, and beating hearts. Trey glanced around. The neighboring lot was taken up by a graying stone church — a mini Notre Dame with flying buttresses, stone gargoyles, and sober-faced saints that looked over the sprawl of Vegas, all but shaking their heads.

Elvis sang on, oblivious to his pious audience, itching and shaking and generally in love.

The muffled purr of a well-tuned engine sounded from the back of the lot. Something fast and feral, full of pent-up horsepower just begging to be unleashed. It revved high then bubbled back to neutral, finally growling into first gear.

25

Gravel crunched. A flash of red swung around the corner, and Trey redirected his gaze, which had been too high. He took in the long, sweeping hood, the set-back cab. His eyes swept over the beady eyes of the headlights, the pinched shark's mouth of a front grill, and the red script of the California license plate. His jaw dropped open as the valet attendant pulled up, slid out, and gave the hood an affectionate pat.

"1962 Jaguar roadster," Elvis sighed, handing him a receipt. "Sweet ride."

"Sweet ride," Trey agreed as he slid behind the wheel and puffed his cheeks out a bit. He ran his hands over the leather-trimmed wheel and admired the chrome-ringed circles of the instrument panel. If he hadn't woken up with Kaya in his arms last night, this might qualify as the most heavenly experience of his life.

His wolf hummed as he eased the clutch into first gear and pulled out onto the road.

Car: check. What the hell should he do now? Still no girl. Still no money. Just a really slick car and a crooning Elvis, going on and on about love.

He pulled onto the road, tapping his fingers on the wheel. Maybe he'd make a plan as he went along.

Something darted through the scene reflected in the rearview mirror, and Trey glanced up. What the hell was that?

A second shadow sliced through the mirror. Something big and toothy, heading straight his way.

An ear-splitting cry sounded, and he ducked a millisecond before the wind whistled over his head. Two giant claws missed the windshield by a hair.

He stared. What now?

Chapter Five

Another *something* flashed overhead, and Trey threw himself sideways. The tires squealed as the car swerved. When he shook his head and popped up, he was in a whole new lane. The oncoming lane.

"Holy sh—"

A Mack truck blared its horn. Trey jerked the wheel right to bring the Jaguar back into the correct lane.

His heart pounded, screaming, *Are you nuts?*

Maybe he was nuts, but he could have sworn. . . He scanned the sky overhead. Without looking, he reached for the radio knob and twisted it to off. The last thing he needed was Elvis distracting him while he was under attack. Attack from—

A hysterical overhead screech, like the sound of nails across a chalkboard, made him duck again. And not a moment too soon, because a jagged claw reached into the open roof of the convertible, grabbing for him as it shot by.

He spun the car ninety degrees across a lane of traffic and down a side road. The smell of burning rubber filled his nose as his shoulder bumped the side panel of the car.

Shit, that had been close — close to getting clawed by whatever-the-hell was attacking him, and close to hitting the flower power VW bus that had been a length behind him in the other lane.

He floored the gas, and the roadster roared off, bringing a crazy grin to his face. At least he had the right wheels for an escape. Low and fast.

The air overhead whooshed, and this time, Trey was prepared. He hunkered down, jerked the wheel, and let his attacker shoot harmlessly by as he finally got a good look.

Not a dragon, which would have been logical, considering the owner of the car.

Not a harpy, either. As easy as that was to picture, this wasn't a bare-breasted beast that was half bird, half furious female.

Nope. None of that. It was a—

He lurched left just in time to avoid another aerial attack by the second... What did you call them? For a moment, his mind refused to cough up the word, until a third beast came screaming by so close, it dinged its ugly black claws against the windshield. And with the ding, the word popped into Trey's mind.

Gargoyle.

Make that gargoyles. Three of them. Big-nosed, ugly-faced, winged monsters that ought to be hunched on the side of a cathedral and not whistling through the rectangle of airspace over his Jag.

He'd seen gargoyles before, but never quite like this. Boston and other historic East Coast cities were full of the things. Ugly bastards just like these, but different, too. The only gargoyles he'd ever come across before were quiet, academic types that haunted Harvard Yard and the parks around the Holy Cross cathedral, tutting over chess games.

Apparently, Nevada had a different breed of gargoyle — as in, the wild, screaming shifters after him now.

Trey slalomed the roadster left and right as they closed in for a second attack. The car was so low, it felt like his head stuck a mile out the open top, so he crouched down, barely able to see over the leather dash. Even then, the first gargoyle to sweep past nearly carved a part into his hair. The second reached lower and scratched a six-inch claw along the trunk before Trey slammed the brakes and let it scrape over the hood.

"Hey!" He winced at the scratch in the paint job. Shit. Kaya was going to be pissed.

Which was ridiculous. Why was he worried about dragon girl being angry at car damage when she was the one who'd flown out on him — with ninety thousand dollars? When he was the one bombarded by flying gargoyles?

His chest tightened a little, though, at the image of Kaya frowning at him. As if getting this right was about a hell of a lot more than just escaping Las Vegas alive. Which made zero sense, because what was more important than surviving?

She is, his wolf rumbled.

He drove along, dodging flying creatures two and three, while a corner of his mind tried to work it out. The gargoyles had hooked on to him the minute he'd driven out of the parking lot, not before. Which meant they weren't after him. They were after Kaya, or at least, her car.

Or were they protecting the car from trespassers like him?

He got his answer half a second later, when two gargoyles swooped in at the same time. The one on the right ripped a jagged gash in the passenger-side headrest, and the one on the left bounced a claw against the rearview mirror, shattering the glass.

So much for the protecting the car theory.

That meant the gargoyles were after Kaya, and that really, really pissed him off. Three ugly-as-sin gargoyles after his auburn-haired goddess? His wolf snarled out loud in a declaration of war.

The first one was back already, and this time, Trey launched his counterattack. One hand, he kept firmly on the steering wheel. The other, he raised, letting his wolf claws extend. All three inches of them — times four fingers. He raked backward as the gargoyle zipped by, digging four parallel lines across the leathery belly of the beast.

The gargoyle screamed, tucked its pointed tail, and peeled off to the side.

"Ha!" Trey allowed himself a little fist pump.

Then the long row of traffic lights that had formed a neat line of green dots turned yellow, then red, and a long, black stretch limo rolled across the next intersection.

And rolled, and rolled, and rolled.

"For God's sake..." He cursed, having no choice but to slow down as an endless expanse of tinted glass flashed by. Man, was that limo long. A couple of tank-topped groupie girls stuck their heads out the skylight in the middle, raising champagne glasses and tossing their hair.

A hook-nosed, ugly-fucker gargoyle whooshed in behind the Jag. Trey cranked the wheel left and caught a glimpse of blazing red eyes as the monster hurtled past him and spun out of control, barely clearing the limo.

Gargoyles were protected by magick that prevented humans from seeing them as anything other than really big, really ugly birds — but that was enough. The party girls screamed and threw their glasses in the air. The gargoyle yelped. Trey hit the brakes and screeched the Jaguar into a hard left turn, nearly clipping the limo as he shot onto a cross-street.

Horns sounded all around as he merged into traffic chugging down his avenue of escape. A pickup coming up from behind careened into a signpost in front of a liquor store, and the SUV behind it slammed into the bumper.

Oops.

Trey retracted his claws, threw the Jag into third gear, and started weaving in and out of cars, trying to gain some ground while his mind spun. How to shake the gargoyles? Preferably without leaving a trail of destruction down Fremont Street. Because, crap, he was on the main drag now. Traffic was slowing ahead, and a glance showed the gargoyles closing in fast.

He beeped the roadster's horn, but no one so much as flinched. A guy on the sidewalk aimed a video camera at the Jag, though, crying out to his wife. "Check it out, honey!"

"Doesn't James Bond drive a car like that?" the high-pitched wife said.

Trey grinned.

"No, Austin Powers did," the husband went on.

Trey frowned and left them behind, accelerating into the tiny space that opened up between two cars, then tucking back into the right lane behind a truck.

Orange lights blinked ahead. A utility company truck was parked beside an open man hole cover, and a guy in a Day-Glo suit waved two lanes of traffic into one.

"Not now..." Trey thumped the dashboard.

Leaning out to see, he found a long line of oncoming traffic closing off the short way around. Meanwhile the gargoyles were closing in fast, and they were not amused. He swept a hand across the dashboard, wishing the Jag came equipped with a rocket launcher. But all it had were the usual instruments, which showed engine temperature, 2500 revs in neutral, and three-quarters of a tank of gas.

Great.

He lifted up a little in the driver's seat and shouted a second before hitting the horn. "Watch out!"

A group of Japanese tourists scattered as he bumped the roadster onto the sidewalk and threw it into second gear.

"I said, watch out!"

Screams filled the air. Limbs flailed. A camera flashed.

Trey kept one hand on the horn and the wheel and the other waving frantically in the air. "Watch out!"

What the humans saw, he had no idea, but they didn't seem to be screaming in horror at the gargoyles so much as screaming at him. Which made him the bad guy, and that really pissed him off.

"Get out of the way!" he yelled again.

A glimpse in the rearview mirror showed the gargoyles coming closer. He had enough of an opening to pull back onto the road, but if he just held on a second longer...

Trey glanced back, then forward, making a thousand calculations in his head. A sidewalk vendor jumped aside, sending a makeshift display of sunglasses flying through the air. A low, steel-frame awning spanned the sidewalk ahead with a huge neon sign that flashed dollar signs and the words, *Win Today!*

One second longer...

He yanked the wheel left so hard, he was afraid the thing would break off. That made the car swing neatly onto the road while the foremost gargoyle smashed full-tilt into the steel sign with a solid crunch.

Trey gunned through the next gap in traffic, opening up his lead again.

He glanced in the rearview mirror. One down, two to go.

Two really pissed gargoyles, but he was on a roll now. He raced past a vintage motorcycle with a side car that he could have sworn carried one of those blow-up sex dolls, and the driver gave the Jag a thumbs-up.

Only in Vegas could a man break a thousand traffic laws and get a hearty thumbs-up for his ride.

He waved back.

Traffic opened up again, and he barreled onward, pushing seventy miles an hour in a thirty zone. He could practically feel the Jag grin.

The air pressure behind him dropped exactly as it had each time a gargoyle dive-bombed him, so he floored the gas and skidded through a hard right at the next intersection.

"Shit!"

A double-decker, open-topped tour bus with a single passenger was coming the other way down Main Street, and the Jag skidded perilously close to the oversized wheels. The g-force of the turn threw Trey into the car door, and for a scary second, he thought the hinge just might give way.

A split second later, the low-flying gargoyle smashed into the tour bus, and the sound of squealing brakes and shattering glass chased him down the road.

He flinched and glanced back to see an open-jawed tourist lean over the side of the bus, gaping at the damage.

The good news: no one seemed to be hurt, except, of course, the gargoyle. Trey grinned. Two down, one to go.

The bad news? The last gargoyle's face was twisted in fury. It bared its teeth and shot forward.

"Shit."

Trey raced for the highway on-ramp not far ahead. He swerved from side to side, trying to shake the monster as it dove at him, again and again. Then he zipped diagonally across three lanes of traffic, hoping the gargoyle would wipe out on a laundry truck, an RV, or one of the other high-profile vehicles on the road. He nearly wiped himself out instead, which sent his heart rate into triple digits. Shifters could survive a lot of damage, but not the kind that came from being dragged under a truck.

He pulled into the right lane and saw green signs flash over-head. Left lane: *Los Angeles, 265 miles.* Right lane: *Reno, 445.*

He huffed. Right, Reno. Like he would ever hit a gambling town again. In fact, he would never play cards anywhere but in a quiet bunkhouse with a couple of buddies way, way out on a ranch.

The gargoyle flattened its ears and thrust forward in what looked like a final, desperate attack. It strained its claws, shaving the hairs off the back of Trey's neck. The ones standing straight up, because he had the Jag going all out with no bright ideas on how to evade the gargoyle now that he'd managed to get boxed in by a couple of trucks.

The gargoyle screamed, reached... and peeled away in a whoosh accompanied by a furious scream.

Trey shook his head, the way he did when his wolf pelt got wet, trying to dislodge the feeling of yet another close call. He craned his neck, catching a last glimpse of the gargoyle arcing back toward the city. He could sense the gargoyle cursing, shaking a fist.

A sign flashed by, telling him he'd cleared Vegas city limits and was now in Paradise, Nevada. And suddenly, the old stories made sense. Gargoyles were stone statues, magicked into life, but only up to strict limits beyond the marble bases they called home.

Trey didn't care about the details. All he knew was that he was clear of the monsters at last.

It took half an hour and nearly fifty miles for his heart rate to settle enough for him to string together a couple of rational thoughts.

Well, not entirely rational, because instead of cutting his losses and driving that sweet roadster straight out to the Pacific coast, he swung right on an unmarked road and followed it for miles. Even when it turned into smooth dirt, he kept going, pulled by some weird sense of direction that told him this was a good way to go. The miles rolled by until Vegas was nothing but a brown smudge in the air to the east. A ridge of dusty gray mountains reared up out of nothing straight ahead, scraping the pale desert sky.

Easing his foot off the accelerator, he let the Jaguar coast to a stop. The sun was inching higher, so he pulled on his hat and listened to the motor bubble for a while. Then he shut it off, got out, and leaned against the front bumper to listen to the wind instead. He closed his eyes and let the sun burn down on him for no particular reason other than it seemed right for that instant in time. His wolf sniffed the open space and the enticing wilderness, folded into the shelter of the mountains.

A shadow passed overhead. He could feel the flicker on his eyelids. The air wavered as it had when the gargoyles had swooped in, but he stood perfectly still. His nose told him exactly who it was.

Not a gargoyle, because gargoyles didn't smell like peach and lavender.

Gargoyles didn't smell like steamy, soul-baring sex, a few hours old.

Gargoyles didn't smell like a sweet, fresh wind out of the pine-filled mountains hundreds of miles north.

Dragons did.

He opened his eyes and watched the red-black dragon scoop its wings, fold them, and settle gently to the ground. Luminous, sea-glass-green eyes looked deep into his.

When he opened his mouth to speak, he made sure it sounded a hell of a lot stronger and steadier than the butterflies fluttering in his stomach.

"Hello, Kaya."

Mine, his wolf rumbled deep inside. *Mate!*

Chapter Six

Kaya stood under the harsh sun of the Nevada desert, staring Trey down. Pretending the same unrelenting magnetism that had pulled them together the previous night wasn't still swirling around her ankles like the beginning of a goddamn hurricane. Pretending they were just a couple of ordinary people on another ordinary day.

Except he looked good enough to eat, dammit, and sounded even better.

Hello, Kaya.

He might as well have said, *Let me lick you right into another orgasm*, the way her body reacted. Pulse racing, blood pooling, face flushing. . .

A damn good thing she was still in dragon form.

She stepped back into the last edge of shade cast down by the edgy hills and clawed the ground. If only she had a little more height. Other than the long neck and tail, she was pretty much the same size as she was in human form. In some parts of the world, there were still dragon shifters that were huge. But for all those in her family tree, shifting didn't actually change body mass, just shape.

She huffed at Trey, trying to produce a little flame.

Of course, she failed miserably, and resented him a little more.

Hello, Kaya, my ass. The only person who'd ever greeted her dragon that casually was her great-grandmother — the one with really poor eyesight and a very absent mind.

She gave her wings a good shake and wiggled her claws for extra effect,. That would show this cocky he-wolf what he was up against. No way could Trey be as cool and collected as he looked. She peered closer and gave a little snort.

His pupils were wide, and his Adam's apple bobbed. So, yeah, she wasn't the only one with a pounding heart here.

She grinned, showing off teeth as long as his fingers.

And what did the bastard do?

He leaned casually against the bumper, as if weary from carrying all those layers of muscle around. Tipping that Stetson of his back, he hooked his thumbs in his jean pockets. His thick brown hair was disheveled in a near-perfect match to the man in her midnight fantasies of the past ten years.

"Good to see you again," he said, as if she'd *agreed* to meet him in the middle of nowhere.

She huffed and lashed her tail.

He grinned.

Grinned, like he started every morning with high-speed car chases and gargoyles. She'd flown over Vegas just in time to see the whole thing from high above, although she hadn't dared show herself in broad daylight. Whatever magick kept humans from seeing the gargoyles certainly didn't cover her. It was enough of a risk to land in this remote corner of the desert and show herself to Trey.

Focus, dammit! Focus!

She shook her head and told herself to get on with her plan, which meant keeping cool, calm, and collected. Her sister's life depended on her, which meant she needed Karen's phone and the number programmed into it. This was about life or death, not the most mind-blowing sex of her life.

Kaya cleared her throat, producing a grumbly dragon growl, and shifted — slowly. Tucking her wings, she retracted her claws and let her scales pull back under her skin. That always burned, but she ignored it, keeping a row of scales down her chest even as the rest of her slid back into human form. It was bad enough to have to negotiate with Cowboy Scrumptious. She sure as hell didn't want to do it naked. Not totally naked, at least.

He stroked his gaze up and down her body as if he wanted to memorize every curve. Almost as if he wanted to live in that moment forever. His eyes glowed. A quick lick made his lips shine, and a little bit of white showed where his top teeth bit down.

Trey's eyes roved a little more, and the glow in them said he was claiming that territory as his own.

"Have a good flight?" he asked.

Her fingers curled into fists, clenching and unclenching just like her teeth.

"That's my car," she started.

He looked back as if he'd forgotten what he'd been leaning against and patted the hood with both hands.

"My car now."

"It's mine!"

The sun slid closer to high noon, and her sliver of shade retreated another inch. They would roast to death if they spent all morning arguing out here.

"How do I know you didn't steal it?"

She stomped a foot. "It's was my grandfather's!"

He didn't even blink. "Seriously? You stole a car from your grandfather? That's just wrong."

She sputtered. "I inherited it when he died, okay? It's mine!"

Damn it, her voice was shaking, the way it usually did when she thought of the kindest, gentlest dragon shifter the world had ever known.

Hot Stuff's smile disappeared as he tilted his head, studying her. He let a minute tick by, giving her the chance to compose herself before speaking again.

"A dragon with a vintage roadster?"

She shrugged. "My granddad retired to Palm Springs after my grandmother died."

The Jaguar was just about the only thing her grandfather had ever indulged himself in, but Trey didn't need to know that. And he definitely didn't need to know what was in the glove compartment.

"The way I see it, this here is my car now." He ran a finger over the chrome edge of the headlight. "Most expensive car I've ever bought. Ninety grand."

A bubble jumped into her throat. Well, of course, he would have noticed the missing cash.

"I need the money."

"So do I," he countered.

"It's important."

He crooked one perfect eyebrow, going from sinfully cute cowboy to smoking hot outlaw. The man could do every flavor of handsome with tiny gestures he probably wasn't even aware of.

She stood as tall as she could. "I saved your life."

"Not sure that's worth ninety grand, sweetheart." He grinned. "And anyway, all I remember is getting jumped by a couple of werebears, then dive-bombed by gargoyles. Not much saving happening there."

"They spiked your drink in the casino. They would have hauled you off to the fighting pits if I didn't... um... If I hadn't..."

She lost a little steam there, searching for words, because she really didn't want to come straight out and say, *If I hadn't dragged you over hill and dale to lose them and taken you to a hotel where I shagged you senseless for most of the night.* Or, *If I hadn't panted over every hard inch of your body the way I've never done with any man.*

"Um... uh...." she stuttered.

"Fighting pits?" he asked, then shook his head, dismissing his own question. "Wait. You don't exactly seem the gambling type. What were you doing in the casino anyway?"

"Like I said, I needed the money."

"Needed to steal *my* money?"

"I can explain." She fidgeted under his gaze.

He crossed one ankle over the other and folded his arms. His eyes charted her long, bare legs, and then he flashed that shit-eating grin. "Be my guest. Explain."

"Dammit, give me a shirt or something." She crossed her arms over her chest. Her dragon skin was itchy as hell, and it was hard to concentrate while hanging on to that last bit of her shifter side.

His wet lips gleamed. "Shy, all of a sudden?"

She winced, remembering some of the sounds she'd made the previous night. The cries. *Oh, Trey! Harder! Deeper!*

"Okay, then you shuck the jeans," she challenged. "Put us on equal footing."

For one horrifying moment, his thumbs twitched in his pockets, and his eyes gleamed. He fingered his collar as if he really were considering stripping there and then.

Her nipples jumped to attention, and her face burned from a blush that must have been beet red. She'd seen her share of naked men, but somehow, Trey set off a whole different set of reactions in her gut. Remembering him naked in the whispering shadows of night was one thing. Drinking in the sight of him in broad daylight...

She exhaled, shooting the air up across her face, trying to cool down.

Finally, Trey relented — thank goodness. He took two steps back, reached into the rear seat, and tossed her a shirt. The bastard even had the manners to look away while she pulled the shirt on. He would be so much easier to despise if he peeked, cackled, or leered. But no, he was playing the gentleman now, all charm and wit.

Damn him, damn him, damn him.

She tugged the hem down as low as it would go.

"Want the pants?" he asked.

She did a double take. How on earth had he managed to grab her clothes while eluding the bounty hunters?

Her pants came flying at her next, landing on her outstretched arm.

"Undies?" He grinned, swinging them on a finger.

She snatched them and yanked them on as he rooted around in a backpack. "I think I have a bra in here somewhere..."

Part of her wished he'd pull out some other woman's bra, because that would make it so much easier to do what she had to do — namely, swindle him out of his money, as well as her phone, her clothes, and oh, yes, the car, too.

But no. He pulled out her black lace bra and held it out like a peace offering. "Yep. There it is."

She grabbed it and stuffed it into her back pocket, then patted the other back pocket. Where was her phone?

"So..." Trey settled against the driver's side door. Blocking it in case she decided to try for a quick escape, he figured. "Explain."

She summoned all the dignity she could. "I don't owe you an explanation."

"No, you owe me ninety thousand dollars," he said with no bitterness whatsoever. "You can give me that instead."

Her shoulders slumped, because he'd just laid the truth bare. She'd robbed an innocent man — well, a man innocent of everything except looking hot as sin and screwing her on the first date when he was drugged. She'd left him to his fate at the hands of a couple of thugs. She'd watched as he'd fought for his life against a trio of gargoyles...

God, what had she done?

"Why do you need a car when you can fly, anyway?" he asked. "And why were those gargoyles after the car?"

She pushed her palms against her eyes, trying to evade reality once again. The gargoyles worked for the thugs who had her sister. They'd picked up Kaya's trail the minute she entered Vegas, and she'd barely shaken them off. They must have been watching the car, waiting for her to return.

A step sounded beside her, and when a gentle hand slid across her shoulders, it took everything she had not to lean in for comfort.

"Hey," Trey whispered. "What's going on?"

She gulped, took a deep breath, then forced her chin up and the truth out.

"I need the car to free my sister. She can't fly."

He tilted his head.

"Half sister." She shrugged. No need to tell him what the other half was... just in case.

He nodded as though the words didn't sound crazy to him at all.

"Is she in some kind of trouble?" His voice went all low and rumbly, like the Lone Ranger about to saddle up and head off on his latest mission.

"You could say that."

She was sniffling now, and dammit, there was no reason for that. Straightening her shoulders, she looked into his eyes — deep, past the compassion and concern, past the worried gleam. Could she trust this man?

The eyes were ocean blue now. *You can trust me.*

She resisted for another moment, then gave in. Who else did she have, if not him?

"My sister came to Vegas a few weeks ago." She shook her head at the memory of the first phone call, in which Karen raved about having a great time and meeting a great guy. "She won some money at the slot machines, then lost a lot more. And more, and more." Kaya winced. God, how could her sister have been so stupid? "Then she borrowed from a guy she'd just met, and lost that, too..."

Trey nodded as she explained. It was all so predictable, really. Except for the details, but she wasn't about to share those.

"Then I got a frantic phone call from her. She's being held by the guy until she gets the money, and if she doesn't get it by tonight..."

Trey's brow wrinkled when she didn't go on. "Then what?"

Kaya fluttered her hands, wishing she could leave the rest out. "He says he'll make her earn it back. The easy way." She made air quotes around *easy*, shivering at the thought of her sister offered up as a sex toy to any paying customer.

Trey's hand caught hers and squeezed just a little bit. "What about the police?"

She shook her head. "These are shifters. We can't involve the police." She hurried on before he asked too many details, such as what kind of shifter was involved. "So I need eighty thousand dollars—"

He groaned and rolled his eyes. "Ninety."

"What?"

He scraped his palms over his stubbly cheeks. "They called this morning, and I had to bluff—"

"You what?" she screeched, jumping away.

41

He shrugged. "The phone rang, some guy demanded money, a woman screamed..."

Her sister had screamed? Kaya's gut clenched.

"I had to do something, so I said they could have five more."

"Five more?"

He nodded. "But the guy went to ten..."

"You were bargaining for my sister?" she shrieked.

"What else was I supposed to do?"

If he hadn't looked so pained, she might have smacked him. She settled for a tiny slap to one muscled shoulder and tried to ignore the little zing the contact sent through her body.

"What did he say?"

He looked up like a chastised puppy. "Midnight. We have until midnight."

She started. *We.* Had he really just said *we?*

"So." He nodded. "What's the plan?"

And just like that, she went from damsel in distress to leader of a rescue squad. A very small squad consisting of one dragon and one wolf.

Make that one nervous dragon and one big, formidable wolf.

She studied his eyes one more time. The same eyes that had held hers in that fairy-tale moment when they'd first met. The very eyes that had thanked her for what she'd done to him — and what she'd let him do to her — last night in bed.

The eyes looking at her now, promising he meant it.

She might just have drowned in those eyes if it hadn't been for him tilting his head and speaking softly. "I'll help. I'm happy to help."

He was the one talking, but she was the one choking on the words. And if Trey was the one who offered a hug, she was the one who leaped into it and wrapped both arms around him tight.

It was crazy, the pull he had on her. Crazy for her to trust him so much. But the whole situation was crazy, right?

She took a deep breath, extracted herself from the hug, and held up one finger. "I'll be right back."

The dreamy look in his eyes was promptly replaced by alarm. "Where are you going?"

She started stripping again. Quickly, before she could re-think her crazy plan. "Hold this. And this." She handed over her pants, then her underwear.

"Um..."

"I'll be right back." She tried to use that sure, cool tone Trey always aced.

She sniffed the air, then jumped. Shifting in midair, she caught an updraft and soared over the hill, telling herself she was not completely nuts. Within five minutes, she was back from the mesa where she'd stashed the loot. She thumped the canvas sack on the hood of the car and retracted her claws. Going straight back to human form, she plucked her clothes out of Trey's arms and yanked them on. Fast.

"Make you a deal, Hot Stuff," she said, trying to sound big and tough.

He crooked one perfect eyebrow and waited patiently, as if he fielded this kind of offer every day.

"Not exactly a fair trade," she admitted. "But it's the best I can do."

"I'm listening."

"Help me get my sister free, and I'll give you the car."

"What if I don't want the car?"

It wasn't a threat. It was a whisper. His eyes were locked on her lips, his expression wistful.

The desert heat pulsed between his body and hers, and her knees wobbled. Exactly the way they had when she'd first laid eyes on him in the casino and felt the blood rush to her head, as if she'd been turning cartwheels or holding her breath too long.

Trey leaned in a little closer, and she stretched until their lips were only an inch apart. An inch too much, so she laid her hands on his chest and reeled him in for a kiss. A kiss that picked up right where they'd left off the night before, and it wasn't long before her leg was climbing his, her hips shoving closer...

It was every bit as good as their first kiss. Maybe even bet-ter, because both of them were clearheaded, or as clearheaded as two people could be with an invisible force zapping around, pushing them together. A perfect kiss Kaya was sure would be etched into her memory forever, if it weren't for the sudden twitch in Trey's ears. His nostrils flared, and his head whipped to the side.

"We have company."

She blinked a little, and when her mind cleared enough to register anything but happiness and warmth, she heard it, too. A car engine. Several car engines, in fact.

Three black Hummers appeared around the bend, and Trey took a step forward, blocking her view.

He tossed the canvas bag onto the back seat of the car, then curled an arm back and shielded her in a protective stance.

"Were you expecting someone?" She craned to see past his shoulder.

He shook his head. "No, but if they saw the gargoyle fight..." He trailed off, but she could fill in the rest. Maybe she wasn't the only supernatural who'd seen the action and followed him all the way out here.

She could feel Trey's pulse race.

"Do you know these guys?"

He squinted at the logo on the side of the vehicles and stiffened. "I know of these guys."

"Good news or bad?" she ventured.

Trey tilted his head left, then right. "I'm not sure yet."

Chapter Seven

Trey kept Kaya close as half a dozen men slid out of the Hummers. Their nostrils tested the air exactly the way his did: wolf sniffing wolf.

And not just any wolves, as the *Lone Wolf* logo on the side of the Hummers told him.

If Trey hadn't have been so busy holding the gaze of the oncoming shifters, he would have slumped in defeat. Everyone had warned him about this cross-country trip, hadn't they? *Keep out of trouble,* his dad had said when he'd first left the East Coast. *Keep out of trouble,* his cousin Lana warned as she waved good-bye from the gateway of Twin Moon Ranch, where he'd worked for a couple of months before continuing his travels in the West.

And here he was, squatting right in the middle of trouble. Thugs, a car chase, dragon lady... He hadn't stepped into trouble so much as dived into it, headfirst.

He shook his head. The dragon lady part, he liked. The rest... Well, the rest was a mess.

An even bigger mess now, because the Lone Wolf Casino was run by Westend pack, and he'd been warned about them. A pack he could have avoided entirely if he'd stayed clear of Vegas.

But, no. There he was, standing firmly beside his she-dragon, pinned by an invisible force he wasn't quite ready to acknowledge.

How had the Westend wolves found him? Well, now that he thought about it, hot-rodding a red sports car through Vegas would have drawn their attention, and he'd left a plume of dust on his way down this dirt road. Plus, if Westend wolf pack was as powerful as he'd heard, they would have shifter spies everywhere. Eagles. Coyotes. Hell, maybe the goddamn jackrabbit he'd nearly run over a few miles back had tattled on him.

Eight big men wearing jeans and white T-shirts formed a circle around him and Kaya and folded their hairy arms. One grunted and showed the points of his teeth.

"Follow us."

An order, not a request, so Trey got in the Jag with Kaya and drove out the way he'd come. They bounced all the way down that dirt road until they eventually rolled onto rough tar and finally onto the highway, all the way back to Vegas. He checked the pale desert sky for gargoyles, but they seemed to have given up on him.

For now, at least.

Faking a casual yawning motion, he reached into the back seat and swept the bag of cash onto the floor, out of sight.

Kaya chewed on her lip. "Who are these guys?"

"Westend wolf pack." He tried to sound casual, as if they were driving along a scenic highway instead of toward an uncertain fate. And as if he hadn't been kissing Kaya back there. Not just kissing, but consuming. Holding. Claiming as his own.

Her brow was furrowed, her fingers busy pushing at the cuticles of her nails. "Good guys or bad guys?"

Exactly the question he was asking himself.

"According to my cousin," he said, "somewhere in between."

She shot him that exasperated look she did so well. "So you don't know them?"

"Not exactly."

"Not exactly?" She threw up her hands.

"Look, I don't know much about dragons. But wolf politics get a little complicated sometimes."

"Complicated?"

"Complicated."

He trailed off as they followed the lead car into an industrial area on the outskirts of the city. Not long after, they pulled up to a huge iron gate that rolled ponderously to one side. He kept the Jag in neutral for a good, long time, not in a hurry to enter, and every last hair on the back of his neck rose.

Crap. His cousin Lana would flay his hide if she found out he'd crossed paths with the Westend wolves. Her Arizona pack and Westend were nominally allies, but it was a working relationship, at best. A rather strained relationship, as he'd gathered over the months he'd spent working at his cousin's place. If Lana — or worse, her mate, the badass alpha of Twin Moon Ranch — found out he was here...

The Hummer behind him revved, signaling him to enter the fortresslike grounds.

"Do you think they'll help?" Kaya whispered.

He forced his fingers not to jitter nervously on the wheel. "If there's something in it for them..."

He looked at her, and her gaze dropped to the floor.

Damn. Clearly, there was nothing in it for these greedy wolves.

A stray thought crossed his mind. What was in it for him?

As if reading his mind, she gripped his hand and whispered, "I'm sorry I got you into this."

Looking into her worried eyes, he realized he wasn't sorry. Not one bit.

"It'll be all right." He tried his best to sound confident. "We have the money..."

There it was again, that heavy *we*. The one that made his wolf hum in satisfaction.

"If they don't find it." Kaya shot a worried look at the back seat.

He shook his head, trying to stay positive. "We have the phone number to set up the switch with the kidnappers — the money for your sister. All we have to do is satisfy this pack that we're not here to infringe on their turf, and then we can concentrate on your sister. Right?"

So easy to say, so hard to do. Especially once the wolves hustled him out of the car, up a grand staircase, and then frisked him in the hallway. They frisked Kaya, too, until he growled so loudly, the guy let her go.

Hands off my woman.

They were led down an ornate hallway hung with cheesy gold curtains with giant gold tassels — the kind he would have loved to fray to pieces as a pup. Kaya walked closer and closer to his side with every step. A set of massive doors opened, and they continued into a huge receiving room where the walls were covered in mirrors and even more gold curtains. A cheap nineties attempt to mimic the palace of Versailles that practically screamed, *Look how rich and successful we are!*

Two steps led to a daislike rise, where a grizzled old shifter sat, glaring at him.

About the only thing this place had in common with Twin Moon pack was the glaring alpha. But the Twin Moon alpha, Ty Hawthorne, exuded an unfailing devotion to his pack. This alpha, from what Trey had heard, had an unfailing devotion to wealth.

The bulky wolf who'd led them in flashed the wallet he'd confiscated from Trey and read from his ID. "Trey Dixon."

Trey winced as the alpha's eyes narrowed on him.

"Dixon?" the man snarled.

Okay, not a good start. He had no choice, though, but to nod.

"Any relation to Lana Dixon?" The alpha crooked an eyebrow.

"My cousin." The less he elaborated, the better. This was already complicated enough.

"And you're here because. . . ?" Roric, the Westend alpha, went on.

Because your thugs dragged me out of the desert and forced me to follow them here? Because I was minding my own business until I met this gorgeous she-dragon, and everything snowballed from there?

"Well, um. . . " He fished for an answer.

"Just passing through," Kaya chipped in.

Her hand trembled in his, though she stood straight and proud as if she faced down powerful alphas every day. She gave Trey's hand a bolstering squeeze that made his pulse race and his heart skip a few beats.

He would jump off a cliff for her, and he didn't even know why. It was scary how quickly his wolf had thrown his lot in with her.

"Just passing through," the alpha echoed, oozing disbelief.

Trey put his hands up. "Honestly. We've just got to take care of one little piece of business and then..."

Roric's eyes narrowed. "Business?"

Kaya rushed to fill in the blank. "I just need to find my sister—"

Find? the alpha's skeptical eyes shouted back.

"Meet! I mean, meet my sister tonight," she hurried on.

The way Roric studied them convinced Trey the less said, the better. No need to complicate matters by mentioning bounty-hunting bears, indebted sisters, or anything else.

"And then we're out of here," Trey added.

Roric glowered with a stare so intense, it just might have lasered a hole through Trey's shirt if another wolf hadn't stepped through the doors, approached Roric, and whispered in the alpha's ear.

Now, what? Trey exchanged glances with Kaya.

"It seems I have pressing business to attend to," Roric growled at last.

"No problem. We'll just get going and—"

"You'll do no such thing," Roric snapped.

Kaya took a step back while Trey glared. Not a smart move with an unfriendly alpha, but he was hardly in the mood to be polite to the guy who'd just snorted at his... his...

Mate, his wolf supplied.

Acquaintance, the human side of his mind insisted.

His wolf snorted and shook his head.

"You will enjoy the hospitality of Westend pack." Roric's tone made the command clear. "I'll deal with you..." He glanced at his watch. "After dinner. Four hours."

He clapped his hands, and two guards scurried forward to lead Trey and Kaya out a side door, where they were immediately intercepted by a curvy brunette. A wee little thing with hungry, appraising eyes that swept up and down Trey's body.

"I'll take over from here, boys," she told the guards.

The two men took half a step back and remained silent.

"I'm Sabrina," she gushed, squeezing between him and Kaya.

Trey's wolf yelped at the unfamiliar warmth at his side. Christ, were those her boobs, mashed up against his ribs?

She all but stroked his ass as she walked along at his side, ignoring Kaya completely.

"Roric is my father." Sabrina smiled a crocodile smile.

Subtext: *You fuck with me, you fuck with my dad.*

Trey forced himself not to shove her away, even though his wolf was snarling inside. Kaya was struggling to keep her claws sheathed. He could feel her anger bubbling up to his left.

Bitch. Kaya's inner curse sounded loud and clear in his mind, and his head whipped around.

Whoa. Had he just heard Kaya's thoughts? Only packmates or destined mates could do that.

She's not a packmate, his wolf filled in smugly. *Which means. . .*

He stared at Kaya, wide-eyed, until something gross and slinky touched his arm. He glanced down to see Sabrina winding her arm through his like she was about to take him for an afternoon stroll. One that would probably end at her bedroom, judging by the way the horny little she-wolf butted her hips against his. Subtext: *And by the way, feel free to fuck me against the nearest wall.*

He looked to the guards. *Uh, guys, a little help?*

The guards just smirked and stared straight ahead.

"You look like you've had a long day." Sabrina patted his chest and cooed like a pigeon. "Maybe you'd like to rest." Subtext: *Feel free to fuck me all afternoon.*

"Um. . ."

She steered him around a corner and down a long hallway.

"Your friend can use this room." Sabrina nodded to an open door. Her eyes brushed over Kaya, saying, *That tramp can use this room.* "And you can come with me to—"

He yanked his arm out of Sabrina's iron grip and darted into the first room with Kaya. He pushed the door shut so fast, he barely had time to squeeze out a few words to Sabrina's shocked face.

"This will be fine, thanks!"

Slam! The door rocked in its frame.

He half expected the young woman to come raging in, but all he heard was the heavy step of a guard and the *click-click* of the door being locked from the outside.

He let out a puff of air and looked around. It seemed all he was finding in Vegas was trouble.

"Now, what?" Kaya asked.

They both turned and took in the suite. There was a platter of cold cuts and bread on a low table, which was nice enough, though the windows beyond were barred. A door led to what looked to be a bathroom, while an alcove held a canopied bed.

King-size, his wolf whistled appreciatively. *For four hours...*

His eyes slid to Kaya just in time to see her gaze jerk to the floor.

Now, what, indeed.

Chapter Eight

Kaya bit her lip and stared at the floor, not sure whether to declare this another up or a down in her roller coaster of a day.

With Trey standing so close, her whole body hummed. That part was a definite plus.

But bars on the windows and a locked door? That part... crap. She shivered at the thought of being trapped. Which was the wrong move, because Trey caught the motion and ran his hand along her arm, sending sparks through every nerve.

"You okay?" he asked in that growly, *I-want-to-feast-on-your-body* tone.

"Fine," she squeaked, skittering away.

God, it was just like the night before, when she'd lost track of her plan the second he stepped too close.

"Um, are you hungry?" She waved toward the platter of food.

Wrong question, because the look in Trey's wolf eyes said, *Yes. Starving.*

Heat pooled low in her body, and she just couldn't drag her eyes off him.

A growl built in his chest, and an electric hum filled the room. Barely audible, like the sound of a thousand mini-bolts of lightning zapping back and forth between their bodies. She leaned forward, and her fingers twitched.

It was just like meeting him in the casino, when it seemed the whole universe had tilted to propel her into his arms. Not that she had fought it. Not one bit.

But this was different. Wasn't it?

She shook her head, trying to free herself from the magnetic attraction that kept pushing her toward him. Her sister was in trouble, a deadline was looming, and now she was captive in a den of wolves. Not the time to be thinking about how good Trey's skin would feel rubbing against hers, or how soft his kisses would land on her bare breast, or how deep he could—

She jolted and practically jumped away. "Um... I'll just... um... ." Her gaze zeroed in on the open bathroom door and the shower stall beyond. "I'll take a shower."

A very cold one.

Before he could protest — and she could see one poised on the tip of his tongue — she fled into the bathroom, closed the door, and leaned against it. Her breath came in pants, as if she'd been chased in there by the big, bad wolf and not her own fears. How far might she go this time, given half a chance? How much of her heart would she hand over and in how little time?

Cold shower. She stripped her socks off quickly. An extremely cold shower, that's what she needed. Followed by a new plan.

Shag him senseless, then break out of this joint? her dragon suggested.

She twisted the tap all the way to the right, shed the rest of her clothes, and stepped in. Yelping at the icy water, she grabbed the shower faucet and willed herself to endure.

It was so cold, her head hurt. Her skin turned bright pink. She lost all feeling in her toes. But the throbbing, achy need deep in her body just wouldn't go away.

She turned the tap to warm. Maybe that would work.

All it did, though, was lull her into a hazy state of mind. She closed her eyes as the shower stall steamed up, telling herself it was the water she was purring at and not the fantasy of Trey's warm touch. Reminding herself that was a bar of soap moving across her body and not Trey's hand.

But then the shower door opened with a quiet whoosh of air-conditioned air, and that wasn't a fantasy. Even without looking, she knew it was Trey — the man she'd only laid eyes on yesterday, but who'd already stolen her heart.

"Kaya."

Somehow, his whisper didn't surprise her. On the contrary, it made her hot all over.

"Kaya," he whispered one more time.

She kept her back to him and gave the slightest nod.

The steam cloud squeezed closer as he moved in behind her and shut the glass door. When he ran his hand down her spine, she nearly purred out loud.

"I think you need some scrubbing back here," he said, so quietly she might have missed it.

Barely moving — barely breathing — she let him pluck the bar of soap from her hand.

"Definitely need some soap back here," he murmured, sliding it down her back.

She squeezed her lips together, trying not to groan at how good it felt, or how hard it made her nipples pucker, or how eagerly it made her sex weep. She tried not to wiggle her ass at him too much and gripped the faucet even more tightly than before.

"Nice," he whispered.

The realization that he was whispering to himself only stoked her inner heat higher.

The soft soap swept around her ribs and eased carefully toward her breast. Trey's callused fingers gave just the right edge to his touch. Because *soft* would only last so long, she knew. Eventually, he'd go over to hard and hot, just like her body was begging him to.

His hand took the weight of her breast, and he circled her nipple, again and again. She arched, encouraging him to work both sides while the hard length of his cock tapped impatiently at her back.

God, she wanted this man. She wanted him like she'd never wanted anything before.

"Trey," she whispered. "That's so good. . ."

A satisfied puff of air tickled her ear, and his cock jutted harder.

"Just what I was thinking," his husky voice promised.

His big, broad foot edged in between hers, and she spread her legs to give him space. Trey scooped a handful of the water cascading over her breast and redirected it downward, toward her mound.

"God, Trey..." she mumbled, pushing backward against his groin.

He caught another handful of water and slid lower this time. Lower...

His left arm, strong and wiry as a tree branch, wrapped around her waist. The fingers of his right hand slid between her legs, parted her folds, and teased.

She threw her head back, murmuring unintelligibly.

"How's that?" He coaxed her along. "Feel good?"

Good was not the word for the skies of heaven, opening up to her in a flash of white light.

He slid two fingers deep and curled them against her inner walls until she yowled like a cat in heat.

"Yeah, that feels good." He nodded. Not a cocky, *look-at-the-power-I-wield-over-you, woman* but a coo of wonder, of discovery. "And what about this?"

She stiffened as a third finger joined the first two. Then she gaped at the ceiling in a silent scream of pleasure she prayed Trey couldn't see. A dragon ought to have some pride, right?

His left hand pushed down against her belly, while the fingers inside curved toward it, intensifying the pressure until she was howling in ecstasy. She grabbed at his hand and pushed harder.

"Faster," she said between clenched teeth. "Deeper."

His breath came in heavy pants, too, as he complied. Two fingers of one hand inside, with a third finger circling her from the other side, while she rattled and cried and shook.

"Trey!"

"Come for me, Kaya," he said in a harsh whisper, like it was him teetering on the edge of orgasm and not her.

She shut her eyes, imagining the hard push of his shaft inside. *Wanting* to come for him, not just for herself. When he scraped his teeth along her neck, she came hard.

Her own groans sounded hoarse and far away, and the whole world shook. Every muscle in her body shuddered in glorious, willing surrender. Wave after wave of pleasure engulfed her until she was limp and weepy in his arms.

One minute, she was dead tired; the next, she spun in his arms with a second wind that had her kissing him harder than she'd ever kissed anyone before. Deeper, with her tongue sweeping in greedy circles and her hands yanking his body against hers.

Her leg was already climbing around his, her fingers gripping tight.

"Okay, cowboy," she panted, popping out of the kiss. "Bedtime."

He crooked an eyebrow. "Bedtime?"

He pulled her leg higher, and for one second, she thought he'd lift her up and screw her right against the wall. Which would have worked, too. But she wanted more than that, like feeling his full weight powering into her.

"Yeah, bedtime. As in, me, you, and the bed."

His fingers gripped her sides harder.

He needed convincing? She'd give him convincing. She dropped her lips to his ear and whispered in a husky voice. "Bed. As in, hot and hard enough to make a missionary blush."

She dropped to her feet as a knowing grin spread across Trey's face.

"Sounds good to me," he murmured, pushing the shower door ajar. "Sounds very good to me."

Chapter Nine

Trey only had the vaguest recollections of their first time the night before, and that was a damn shame. Practically criminal, like sleeping through Christmas, New Year's, and his birthday, all in a row.

So he watched, listened, and sniffed, memorizing every detail. Tiny drops of water cascaded down Kaya's body as he lowered her to the bed. Her eyes shone, and her fingertips dug into his arms. The scent of her arousal mixed with his, creating a potent cocktail that made his wolf howl.

"You coming, wolf?" Her feet ran along the outsides of his thighs in a tease.

Oh, he was coming, all right.

"You'll be the one coming," he murmured. "Very, very soon."

Her breath came faster and harder, and he thanked heaven for making dragons as horny as wolves.

But, hell. Where to begin?

His cock and balls voted to get right to work, while his wolf screamed for a closer sniff of her neck, and his hands begged for more of those perfect, pert tits.

He shoved those thoughts aside, because there was only one right way to start this.

With a kiss.

A slow one. For all that his body was screaming to skip ahead, his soul needed that one kiss.

He slid up her body, cupped her face in both hands, and lowered his lips. Closing his eyes, he drank in the sigh that escaped from her even before he touched down. A second later, it was him sighing at the sensation of that perfect fit. Her

59

lips slid sideways, then opened, and God, she tasted so good. Like peaches. Like honey. Like sunshine, almost. Her hands stopped roving and stayed on his ribs, and the only things that moved for the next minute were their pounding hearts and their lips.

Until, at some point, he could practically feel his wolf lean in and tap on his shoulder to say, *Hey, buddy. You got your one kiss. Now I get mine.*

At which point the kiss became a frenzy for more, more, and more that Kaya's dragon seemed just as happy to run with.

"Tell me what you want," she gasped between deep, hard kisses. "Tell me what you like."

"I want you," he mumbled, sliding down her body to kiss her neck.

Want to lick, his wolf added. *To pinch, just a little bit. Maybe even nibble—*

He yanked on an invisible leash and slid farther down her body, ignoring his wolf's protest.

I was just sniffing! his wolf protested. *I swear!*

He shook his head. That this was more than just good sex — really, really good sex that made his heart and soul soar — was clear. But there was no way he was going to let his inner wolf grab the chance to do something rash. If there really was truth to the notion of destined mates—

Of course, there is! his wolf hissed.

And if Kaya really was his destined mate—

Of course, she is!

They would talk about it later, like a couple of rational adults, not hot-blooded shifters.

Talk? his wolf scoffed. *What is there to talk about?*

Everything. Like how the hell could a wolf and a dragon make a life together...

How the hell can we not *make a life together?*

He struggled for an answer to that one. For once, the wolf had him stumped.

Well, whatever. He shoved the beast aside. All of that was for later. Right now was for letting their bodies get to know each other the very best way. And for memorizing every smooth curve, every soft line, every hard ridge of her body.

"Tell me what you want me to do," Kaya whispered, running her hands over his shoulders.

He dropped lower, kissing her collarbone. Her chest rose with deep, needy breaths.

"This." He kissed his way down to her breast. "I want this."

"This?" The word turned into a squeak as his lips caught her nipple.

He licked in circles, letting his body weight pin her down.

"This." He nodded. "I want you to lie back and let me explore."

She answered with a needy moan.

"I want to study every inch of you." He nibbled at the underside of the plump flesh.

Kaya sighed in pleasure, lifting him with her long inhale.

"I want to touch you. Everywhere."

Her knees flopped apart in open invitation, and his wolf howled.

He nosed her belly, inhaled deeply, and dropped between her legs.

The night before, he'd been drugged by some chemical. But now, he was drugged on the scent of her skin and on the arousal wafting from every pore. On the crazy little mewing sounds Kaya made when he parted her folds and let his tongue dive in.

She might have been a dragon, but she sure did cry like a kitten when he turned her on.

He glanced up. "Is that good?"

Her hands clutched the sheets. Her head was tipped back, and her breaths came in gasps.

"I'll take that as a yes," he chuckled and ducked back in.

"Trey..." She pulled at his shoulders. "I'm so close."

He swept his tongue upward in one last, openmouthed taste. He was close too — so close, it hurt.

"Please." When she lifted her head, the line of her abs rose like a mountain ridge. "Inside. I need you inside."

He dragged himself away from heaven to shuffle up along her body.

"Ready?" He nudged her legs wider to make space for his cock.

Kaya shook her head, but an indulgent smile slipped over her lips. "Like you have to ask."

∞∞∞∞

Kaya clamped her legs around Trey, as ready as she'd ever been in her life. More than ready, because her mind was already two steps ahead, imagining the hot slide of him inside.

When he did, she gasped. He was so wide, so hard, and the pain was so, so good. Skin-on-skin, because she really didn't give a damn about a condom right now.

She moaned when he snuck in another half inch, then half an inch more. Thick, muscled arms criss-crossed with a hundred chiseled lines of muscle caged her in. His legs trembled, and she felt him struggle with his inner wolf to give her time.

She didn't know what kind of partner he was used to — and she sure didn't want any details, either — but if he thought dragons needed *slow* and *careful*, he had another thing coming.

She moaned, clawing his back. "Deeper." Dammit, she was begging now. But really, how could she resist?

All the air went out of her as he plunged in. A *you-asked-for-it, you-got-it* dive that ended with his hips slamming against hers and him buried deep, deep inside.

"Kaya," he sang.

She clamped down on him with her inner muscles, wishing she could capture the sound he made. No one said her name that way, making it into its own melody. No one.

"Kaya," he whispered.

His voice was hoarse that time, and it still sounded good. But they weren't lying in that bed to sing, or to whisper, or to cry, so she licked her lips and forced out two words.

"Again," she ordered. "Again."

He angled his hips to the right and thrust back in, riding one wall of her core hard. Pulling back out, he angled left, then pushed in again, doing the same to the other side. Out and back, out and back, always with that delicious, diagonal slide that made her hungrier. Wider. Wilder.

She dug her heels into his ass and danced with him, leaning left and right to accentuate each move in a sensual waltz. The last rays of sunlight flickered in through the window and over the walls. The suite became a time machine, throwing her way, way back in time to caveman days, when primitive instincts could take over and conscious thought could retreat, at least for a little while. Just her and that wolf, possessing her. Thoroughly.

She closed her eyes to the delicious, searing heat of his movements. Focusing on giving as good as she got, she squeezed down inside, matching his moves.

Was she doing it right? She peeked. If Trey clenching his teeth, closing his eyes, and murmuring her name was any indication — then, yeah, she was doing pretty well.

So she did it again, rippling over him like a vise as he thrust forward, dragging moan after audible moan out of the man doing the same to her.

Teetering on the edge of an incredible high, she called his name.

His body was bent so low over hers that the sweat starting to gleam on his chest didn't drop so much as slide over to her. And dang, even that felt good. Impossibly good. Unbearably good.

"Trey..." Her voice wavered until she couldn't hold back. Wave after wave of sensation steamrolled over her. Emotions, too, dammit, including a desperate, sentimental longing for something she couldn't quite name.

Mate, her dragon puffed inside. *My mate.*

He grunted and went stiff all over, filling her, and she squeezed every appendage around him, keeping him close.

Her heart thumped. His breath came in shallow pants. The throb in her chest could have been Trey's pulse or her own. His fingers tightened around hers, just as they'd done the night before, and a languid kind of peace washed over her as he collapsed, then turned and wrapped her in his arms.

Mine, her dragon purred. *Mine.*

She really ought to have stamped such crazy thoughts away, but she just couldn't muster the willpower. Resisting him was useless. And, hell. Temptation had never felt this good or this right.

"Mine," he murmured, and she snuggled closer, crossing her arms over his.

A lifetime passed in a minute, and she didn't regret a thing. She just wrapped herself tighter in the blanket of his warmth and hung on to a high that lifted her body and soul.

"Wow," she murmured, which was short for, *Hot damn, that was good.* Maybe she should have hooked up with a wolf sooner.

She laughed in spite of herself. As if she had a huge stable of gorgeous, steel-muscled he-wolves to choose from back in her remote Wyoming home. As if she'd ever met a man like this before.

After one kiss to his arm, she squeezed her eyes shut. She never needed to go looking anywhere else, ever again.

"What?" He tapped her shoulder, and she rolled around. Then she popped a kiss smack on his lips. One tiny kiss to follow the hurricane-force winds that had just swept past, but it stood out all the same. Love amidst lust. Poetry amidst passion.

She squeezed her lips together, holding on to his taste. "You... I mean, us. I mean, this..."

The corners of his eyes crinkled into a smile. "I think I know what you mean."

Did he? She searched his face for any hint of a lie or a rote line, but there was none of that. Just joy and wonder and... wow, fearlessness.

She took a deep breath, settling her nerves. Well, the few restless nerves that still had the energy to flutter inside her body. The rest were already snoring in bone-deep contentment. Maybe those were the ones she ought to trust, instead of the nail-biting, doubting ones over there. Was it really possible for love to move this fast?

"Hey," he whispered, tugging her against his chest.

She laid an ear against his skin and listened to the sure, steady beat of his heart.

"I don't get this, either." His voice was deep and rumbly from that close up. "But there's something my mom used to say..."

She tilted her chin up and found his eyes.

He smoothed her hair back, tucking it behind her ears. "Sometimes, you just got to trust."

Slowly, she rested her head against him again. She liked the sound of that. A lot.

"You want to hear my dad's version of that?" she asked a moment later, punching through the feeling of possibility that had settled over both of them.

"Sure. What?"

She dropped her voice to match her father's gravelly bass. "Never, ever trust anyone. Especially a man."

Trey laughed, and the movement bounced her around. "What about a wolf?"

"Ha." She rolled around to lie flush over his body, head to toe, making the mattress dip even more. "He never said anything about wolves."

"There you go." Trey pointed right at her, like he'd known it all along. His eyes shone as he echoed his own words. "There we go."

We. A word to frame and clutch to her chest forever, if she hadn't been clutching him.

He rocked her a little, and she sighed. "So tell me something, wolf."

"Anything," he answered without the slightest delay.

"Tell me..." She searched for whatever it was she was dying to find out. But what did she need to know about the man that he hadn't already shown her in word and deed? "Um..."

He chuckled and started humming a game show theme. "Waiting, darlin'."

He was mimicking that drawl, so she started there. "Where are you from?"

"Massachusetts."

Her head popped up. "Massachu..."

65

He laughed. "Disappointed?"

She shook the notion away.

"I've been working in Arizona lately," he explained. "On my cousin's ranch."

So that's where the cowboy part came from.

"Is that where you learned to play poker?"

His eyes sparkled with mischief. "Among other things."

Huh. She'd lived most of her life in Wyoming, and she'd never really wanted to leave. What about him?

"Why did you leave home?"

"Dunno. I just wanted... something else." His gaze flitted vaguely over the room, bouncing from curtains to ceiling to bedside lamp until it landed on her. And just like that, his eyes dialed into sharp focus. His breath caught on something, and his Adam's apple bobbed.

Kaya's heart thumped, seeing him look at her that way.

He dragged his eyes away, and damn, she would put good money on the fact he'd just figured out what *something* might be.

Dragon lore was full of mysterious forces, like fate, destiny, and serendipity, but none of them was ever used to explain love. Fate was the collective head-shaking that came after a dragon plowed into a cliff at night and crashed to his doom. Destiny was the shrug that came with a business enterprise falling apart. Serendipity was the punchline of a joke told by two dragons at exactly the same time.

Love, on the other hand, was a couple of dragons getting it on late on a Saturday night.

None of those words, seemed strong enough to explain *this*. Not even *destiny*.

But wolves, from what she'd heard, believed in those terms the way zealots believed in prophets and gods. Wolves were legendary for spending lifetimes sniffing after scents they swore stemmed from destiny. For bachelors deciding from one day to the next that it was time to settle down. For spending lifetimes gazing into each other's eyes and howling nighttime duets.

Wolves, as her grandfather used to say, were a mystery.

Love, as her mother said, was a mystery.

She stared into Trey's eyes, shining like the moon over the sea.

Then he cleared his throat, murmured something about cleaning up, and disappeared into the bathroom.

Trey. Wolf. Man.

All in all, a mystery.

Chapter Ten

Four hours. They had four hours.

The first two, they spent gazing into each other's eyes, boinking like bunnies, and cooing like a couple of lovebirds.

Then they spent an hour trying to figure out what the hell to do next. Midnight wasn't getting any further away, after all.

The final hour, they went back to shagging, cooing, and clinging blindly to hope in that little den of a room, because the world was easier to understand that way.

Trey climbed out of the shower for the second time in four hours and yanked his clothes on just in time to hear the heavy lock click. Two wolf shifters opened the door and tipped their heads down the hallway in an unmistakable order.

He grabbed Kaya's hand and hung on to it as they were marched all the way back to the place he'd started thinking of as the throne room.

There wasn't a window anywhere. Not even a clock — just a lot of gold-edged mirrors that mocked every step he took. The place was like a casino, just a lot quieter.

And somehow, he didn't have the feeling he would walk out of this den a winner.

Shit, shit, shit. A few hours ago, he and Kaya had everything they needed: the money and the phone number. All they had to do was call the man holding her sister for ransom and set up the switch. All so simple — if only they could get away from these wolves.

The reflection in the mirror taunted him. *Did you really think it was going to be easy?*

A gnawing sense of dread grew in his gut, and he tugged Kaya closer until her shoulder bumped against his with every anxious step.

"Dixon." A voice growled at him, and his head snapped up. Roric, the alpha, was glaring down from his dais like a medieval king.

He nearly growled back. If he'd been alone, he might have played the role of subordinate to this powerful man. But with Kaya there, stubborn alpha instincts took over. The instinct to protect. To throw out his chest and make a stand. To show he would not be pushed over.

He stared back, and the reigning alpha's gaze locked him in place.

"Here I was, thinking we had just another couple of visitors..." Roric paced like a restless lion, looking for a way out.

Not a promising start.

Kaya's fingers tightened over Trey's as Roric nodded to himself. "So I made a few phone calls..."

Trey hid a grimace. Shit.

"Seems that Lana Dixon of Twin Moon Ranch has no idea her cousin is visiting my territory."

Good news in one way, because at least Trey had a chance of keeping Twin Moon pack out of the trouble he'd stumbled into. Bad news, because it made him a lone wolf, with no one to cover his ass.

His stupid ass. Had he really thought he could roll in and out of Vegas a couple of thousand dollars richer without being noticed?

He went for the truth. "I was hitchhiking to LA and the driver let me out here."

Ignoring him, Roric paced on. "I give my regards to Lana, hang up the phone, and what happens next?"

Trey glared in the heavy pause that ensued. How the hell did he know?

"It seems someone else is calling me at the same time, wondering what motherfucker wiped out his gargoyles." Roric threw an icy look at Trey. "No, wait. He was wondering what motherfucking *wolf* wiped out his gargoyles. Asking if it was one of mine."

Shit. He hadn't just annoyed the Westend alpha, he'd stepped on his toes.

"So I got to wondering if that wolf has anything to do with the wolf who wandered in here, you know?"

Trey clenched his jaw. It wasn't as if he'd wandered willingly into this screwed-up wolf den.

"And, meanwhile, it seems the little lady has trouble of her own." Roric sneered at Kaya.

She stiffened, and Trey did too. Little lady?

"Seems the lady owes money to an associate of mine."

Kaya's fingers dug into Trey's as her lips formed a thin line. Maybe she was like him, biting back her inner beast's teeth before they could extend out of her gums.

"The same associate, as it turns out, whose gargoyles were damaged."

Damaged, like they'd chipped a nail and not run head-on into a bus or a steel frame.

"So what's a wolf to do?" Roric's stiff posture made it clear he wasn't expecting an answer. Finally, he sighed in a way that said, *So much work in my little fiefdom, so little time.* "So I decided to invite my associate over and get this misunderstanding settled, once and for all."

Now, why didn't Trey like the sound of that?

A tall, dark figure with a sleek black ponytail stepped out of the shadows on the left side of the hall. He wore a tailored, black-on-black Armani suit that made his pale skin seem almost translucent. His eyes instantly dismissed Trey, but lit up as they prowled over every inch of Kaya's body.

Her hand trembled in his, and all Trey could do was hang on. A growl built in his throat.

"Miss Proulx, I presume," Roric's associate said in a light European accent of some kind. He gave a tiny bow, like he was a god damn count or something. When he straightened and smiled, the points of his teeth showed.

Kaya gasped in recognition.

A second later, Trey caught on, too. Those weren't teeth. They were fangs. Vampire fangs. The guy who was holding her sister for ransom was a goddamn vampire?

Trey sniffed the air and found it void of any scent — the hallmark of a vampire. A real-life, pointy-fanged, bloodsucking vampire.

He glanced at Kaya. *Tell me you just forgot to mention the vampire part.*

She shot back an apologetic glance that said, *Minor detail.*

Minor detail? Her sister wasn't just indebted to some Vegas gambler, but to a vampire gambler. Vampires were sneaky, conniving creatures who could suck even the strongest wolf dry of life. Vampires fought dirty and preyed on the weak.

And yet, this one was somehow associated with the Westend wolves. Trey glared at Roric. How could any wolf stoop so low as to deal with vampires?

Roric gave him a merciless shrug that said, *Business is business, son.*

It was just as Lana had warned him. Westend pack fostered a mercenary attitude uncommon among wolves.

"I've heard so much about you," the vampire said to Kaya. "We've been waiting so eagerly for your visit." His eyes caught on her chest, and a scarlet-red tongue licked his pale lips.

A second vampire appeared behind him, then a third, shoving a stiff captive along.

"Get your hands off me, asshole," the woman grunted.

"Karen!" Kaya darted forward.

Trey caught her arm and yanked her back. No way was he letting Kaya close to a vampire. They were already much too close. As in, a thousand-mile radius kind of close.

"Hi, Kaya," Karen sighed, twisting out of the vampire's grasp. "Sorry I got hung up with half of fucking Transylvania here." She rolled her eyes and made a mockery of their names. "Igor and Ivan."

The brunette who looked so much like Kaya exaggerated the vowels — *Ay-gor and Ay-van* — and the vampires rolled their eyes.

GAMBLING ON HER DRAGON

"Ee-gor," the first corrected her, clearly not for the first time.

A little smirk slipped onto Karen's lips. "Whatever."

Boy, was she feisty. Just like her sister.

"We have the money," Kaya blurted. "We were bringing it to you."

"Oh, yes?" Igor, the head vampire, raised a thin eyebrow.

"Actually, I have the money," Roric smirked, holding up the bag of cash his men must have brought in from the car.

"That's my money!" Kaya and Trey blurted in unison.

"My money, now." Roric grinned.

"You wouldn't!" Kaya barked.

Roric raised his eyebrows in challenge. Of course, he would.

"Money I'm happy to give my associate to reimburse him for his losses." Roric shot an accusing look at Trey. "Minus, of course, a small fee for rescuing you out there in the desert."

"Rescue?" Kaya sputtered.

Trey growled openly. So he'd inadvertently messed with whatever tenuous pact Roric's pack had with the vampires. Surely, wolves would stand together when the going got tough?

Roric shook his head. *Fat chance, kid.*

Igor flicked a fleck of lint off his sleeve and sighed. "Reliable gargoyles are so hard to find these days. And the price witches charge for new ones..."

"All in the name of maintaining smooth business relations, of course." Roric shrugged at Trey's incredulous look. *Yes, these vampires are snobs, but what can you do?*

Trey shook his head. Back home, wolves and vampires gave each other a wide berth, just in case. But this was Vegas and the shady Westend pack. Why was he not surprised?

Igor brushed a delicate lace hanky against his nose. *Heathens*, his dismissive look said.

"That's our money!" Kaya stretched to her full height. Her eyes flashed, and Trey wondered if she would start breathing fire. A trick that would come in awfully handy at a time like now.

He bared his teeth at the vampires, backing her up. Really, he ought to be correcting her. Technically, it was *his* money, but somehow, he didn't care. The line between what was Kaya's and what was his was going gray and blurry, like none of that mattered as long as they stood together — and stayed together.

Forever, his wolf hummed.

"Such a pity," Igor tsked, fingering Karen's hair. "But I'm sure your sister will be happy to earn back what she owes me in a different way."

Karen yanked out of his grip and snarled. "Over my dead body."

Igor gave her an icy smile. "That would be the hard way, my dear. But that, too, can be arranged."

The vampires behind him licked their lips.

Karen smirked. "You think you boys can drink pure dragon blood? All that mercury in my veins..." She let the words hang in the air like a threat. "I doubt it."

Trey glanced at Kaya. Hadn't she said Karen was a half sister who couldn't fly? That meant Karen was only half dragon and probably didn't have the high mercury content that protected purebred dragons from vampires.

Karen stood proud and unwavering, playing the world's most dangerous bluff with a perfect poker face. Trey wondered how she'd ever lost whatever bets she'd made to get into trouble in the first place.

The corner of Igor's eye twitched as he struggled to keep his cool. Clearly, Karen hadn't been as cooperative a captive as he had imagined. More like the *Ransom of Red Chief*-type — the little boy who drove his captors so crazy, they ended up paying his family to take him back.

"The most noble of vampires can drink dragon blood." Igor leaned in menacingly. "And it can be distilled. Remember, my dear: the easy way, and the hard way..."

"I'll show you the hard way," Karen muttered, clenching a fist.

Trey stepped forward before she swung it. "Forget it."

Igor laughed. "And what exactly do you have to bargain with?"

Trey stopped just short of shaking a clenched fist in the vampire's face. Crap, what did he have?

"The car. You can have the car."

"Granddad's car?" Karen squeaked. "No way."

Kaya shook her head in a vehement *No,* and Trey stared at the two of them.

Igor let out another annoying tut-tut sound. "I have all the cars I need."

Kaya cast a wild glance around the room, desperate for some bargaining chip. Trey socked Roric with a beseeching look. Surely, the old wolf...

Roric snorted and motioned his guards forward. *Clear my hall of this rabble,* he might have commanded, if Igor hadn't spoken first.

"Of course, there might be one thing..." Cool, appraising eyes traced every inch of Trey's bulk.

He felt the cold hand of death creep up and down his spine as he wondered what Igor had in mind.

"Two of my scouts reported spotting a new candidate for the pits," Igor murmured. "I wonder if that could be you."

Kaya froze at his side. "No. No way."

Trey tilted his head at the vampire. The pits?

"No!" Kaya grabbed his arm. "Not the pits."

She looked so deeply into his eyes, he nearly obeyed the unspoken command. *Don't do it. You can't risk it.*

Igor coughed in a not-too-subtle hint, and Trey dragged his eyes away from Kaya to her sister. Somehow, he had to get the two of them free. And, hell. He could fight as well as any wolf. Better, even. And since he didn't have any better ideas...

"Don't," Karen warned.

But what else could he do?

"Let's say I fight," Trey proposed, turning to the vampire. "And I win. Then we go free. All three of us."

Igor's eyes were a dull, flickering red that hurt to look at. Trey hung on, though, straining every muscle to do so. He could stare this ass down. He could fight and win.

He had to.

Igor's pale lips parted in a mockery of a smile. "Agreed." He said it so quickly, Trey wondered what he'd just gotten himself into.

"And the car," Kaya shot out. "We get the car, too."

Trey blinked at her. Boy, she sure had a thing for that Jag.

And a thing for him, apparently, because the squeeze she gave his hand a moment later came with a husky whisper. "I owe you, my wolf."

His heart soared a little like Kaya had, that night off the balcony. That crazy night that started this whole wild day. A day he wouldn't go back and change any part of if it meant losing her.

He swallowed the lump in his throat and told himself to concentrate. Fight first. Mate later.

Mate, his wolf hummed. *My mate.*

For the first time, his human side didn't bother protesting. It just hummed right along. *Mate. My mate.* That had a certain ring to it, now that he'd gotten used to the idea.

Igor snapped his fingers at one of his men, who pulled out a phone. "Rearrange tonight's schedule." He turned to Trey with a grin. "Come along, then. No time to waste."

One of the vampires grabbed Karen, who elbowed him in the ribs but gave in when a second vampire clamped a hand over the back of her neck. "All right, already..."

Roric chuckled. "Funny how I just happen to have some cash on hand for a bet." He thumbed through the wad of cash he'd pulled from the canvas bag. "Who's fighting tonight?"

"Kyrill," the second vampire said.

Roric whistled. "Sure money."

Kaya gaped at him with wild eyes. *Sure money for whom?*

Trey shook off the sinking feeling in his gut. Everything was coming together in perfect symmetry, but it was a fucked-up kind of symmetry. The cash he'd won had brought him together with Kaya, and now, that same cash was being bet against his life. All three of their lives, because Kaya's and Karen's fortunes were riding on his shoulders, too.

He took a deep breath. Fate was definitely toying with him. The question was, did it plan for them all to meet a happy or a tragic end?

Chapter Eleven

Kaya half stepped, half stumbled out of the vampires' chrome and leather SUV. A neon light flashed in her eyes, setting off every inner alarm. She'd never been so tempted to shake out her wings and fly the hell home.

Scarlet Palace, the casino sign announced.

"Home sweet home," one of the vampires murmured.

Kaya held her chin high, keeping herself together. She desperately wished to have Trey at her side, but he'd been thrown into another vehicle and taken on a different route.

Seeing him go was like waving good-bye to home, family, and every fond memory, all at the same time. Maybe wolves weren't crazy to believe in mates, after all.

She forced herself to take a deep breath. She had to keep her cool and figure out how to get out of this mess.

"Get moving." The vampire shoved her forward.

Like a prisoner sentenced to life, she took a last gulp of fresh air and stumbled through the double glass doors.

The sound of jazz music hit her ears, and the scent of fresh greenbacks and rum invaded her nose. Her eyes hurt from all the flashing lights, hysterically begging for attention.

"It's like Christmas on steroids," Karen muttered. "Can you believe I survived here for a week?"

"I can't believe you got into this mess in the first place," Kaya growled. She loved her sister, but damn, this time, Karen had really bitten off more than she could chew.

"I'll explain later," Karen whispered in a strangely determined voice that made Kaya look twice. What was there to explain?

Igor waved a pair of bouncers aside and led the way to a bank of VIP elevators. There, he tilted his head toward the open doors. "Ladies."

"Blood-sucking vampires," Karen muttered, digging in her heels.

Kaya dragged her sister in. "Do you have to provoke them?" she hissed while Igor barked orders outside the door.

Karen wiggled free. "Show these assholes an inch, they'll take a yard."

Kaya was thinking more along the lines of *They'll take a few gallons of your blood,* but she kept her lips sealed.

Igor strode in with two of his henchmen, one of whom slotted a key into an unmarked space on the control panel below all the other buttons. The elevator started its descent.

Kaya counted fifteen floors, judging by the periodic rumble outside the doors as they dropped and dropped and dropped. Fifteen floors below street level?

The doors pinged, and Karen sighed, "Welcome to the lowest circle of hell."

Kaya stepped forward, then halted at the sound of a cheering crowd coming from down a dark hallway. At a shove from Igor, she followed Karen and the vampire to an usher's station, high above an open arena. A rabid crowd of several thousand pointed down at the circle of sand. There, two figures crouched in a circular area. At first, Kaya thought it was a boxing ring. Then she realized it was a gladiator's pit, delineated by a stone wall topped with faux-Roman statues of gods and emperors.

"Whoa. Are we in Vegas or ancient Rome?" Kaya wondered out loud.

"The basic principles of entertainment haven't changed in two thousand years," Igor commented with a bored wave of the hand. His breath tickled Kaya's ear, and she scurried forward. He'd been crowding her ever since they'd left the Westend wolf den. His eyes traced the long line of her legs and studied the rise and fall of her chest. The vampire might not be able to suck her mercury-rich dragon blood, but there were other ways he could hurt her.

She glanced around. She, Karen, and Trey had to find a way out of there, and soon.

A commentator's voice blared through speakers, but she didn't catch a word.

"The Annihilator is on." One eager spectator read to another from a printed program as Kaya brushed past.

The crowd broke the name into syllables and cheered in a bone-chilling cry for blood.

"Right this way, ladies." Igor pointed to a red carpet that led to a sectioned-off booth.

"I'll *lady* him right in the balls, first chance I get," Karen muttered under her breath.

Karen, the tomboy. Karen, the wisecracker. Karen, who was likely to get them all killed.

"Stop that," Kaya hissed.

Igor motioned them into the plush seats beside his. Each was big enough for Kaya to lose herself in on a lazy weekday night with a bowl of popcorn, a good movie, and a good man.

Like Trey. A vision of being snuggled up with him on a quiet Wednesday night set off little sparks until Karen popped her bubblegum and dragged Kaya back to grim reality. No snuggling. No peace. No Trey.

She perched on the very edge of her seat and studied the scene. Damn it, where was he?

The popcorn gobbled by greedy spectators was about as far as the similarity to her fantasy went. There was no peace in this hellhole, just a primitive thirst for blood, pulsing under the surface of the wild scene.

"Ice cream! Beer! Lemonade!" A broad-shouldered salesgirl hefted giant beer glasses and flashed her cleavage, Oktoberfest-style.

"Place your bets! Get 'em in now, ladies and gents, get 'em in now!" A thin man in a pinstriped suit smoothed back a lock of his slicked-back hair. Kaya sniffed and found a clear hint of something canine in his scent.

Another wolf? She looked at her sister.

"Hyena," Karen answered without a second glance. "They handle all the bets. The bears do security..."

Kaya looked up at the burly men guarding each aisle, clad in orange safety vests. Yeah, they were bear shifters, all right. One of them hustled an overeager woman back to her seat, while another bared his teeth at a man trying to sneak down toward a ringside seat.

"But how..." Kaya started.

Karen nodded upward, past the stage lights. "The witches cast just enough magick over the pits to make sure the human part of the audience only sees what they want them to see — either humans or animals, but nothing in between."

Kaya squinted past the glare of lights to a glass booth high in the eaves of the arena, where she spotted three old women with blue-tinted hair. Witches, for sure. One buffed her nails. Another leafed through the pages of *People* magazine. The third yawned and briefly put aside her knitting to peer over the crowd.

"Watch," Karen said.

The witch sat straighter, and Kaya followed her gaze to a section of the crowd thick with humans. Among them was an elk shifter, apparently too caught up in watching the fight to remember to conceal his animal side. His antlers were starting to show, and a woman in the row above his — a human in a sequined top — opened her mouth to scream. The witch fluttered her fingers in a quiet spell, and a moment later, the human shook her head, dismissing the crazy vision, and turned her attention back to the action in the ring.

The witch gave a satisfied nod and went back to knitting.

"See what I mean?" Karen said.

Meanwhile, in the fight pit, two figures closed in on each other. A lion and a grizzly, growling up a storm.

"Here, pussy, pussy," the bear goaded his foe. Kaya heard the words coded into his roar.

The crowd cheered and Karen bent close to Kaya's ear. "The humans only see the animal side of the fighting shifters. They're supposed to stay in one form or another, but they sometimes slip."

The lion snarled. "Son of a bi—" he started with words and ended in a roar.

No one blinked an eye, and a glance up at the witches in the control booth showed one winking at another.

"I thought animal fights were illegal," Kaya said.

Karen just rolled her eyes. "This is the side of Vegas the law doesn't touch. Anything goes."

That, Kaya had to agree with. The last few days in Vegas had proven that again and again.

"What other spells can the witches cast?" she asked.

Karen pooh-poohed the notion. "Not much, believe me. Third-rate witches."

Igor sighed. "Good witches are so hard to find."

"My heart bleeds for you," Karen shot back.

He grinned. "That, too, can be arranged."

Kaya elbowed her sister in the ribs and tugged her away. Far away.

A mighty roar cut off whatever smart-aleck response Karen had ready, and the crowd jumped to its feet. Kaya did too, in spite of herself, watching the lion and grizzly fly at each other in a blur of fur and fangs.

The grizzly howled in pain as the lion scraped four parallel lines into his back and jumped clear.

"Whoa. Do they fight to the death?"

"Nah," Karen replied all too casually. "Not in this round."

Kaya dug her fingers into the seam of her seat cushion. Shit. What round was Trey in?

She looked away as the lion closed in on the staggering grizzly.

The crowd cheered. The grizzly moaned. The lion roared in triumph. Kaya figured death would be swift, but a shrill whistle blew, and a gang of handlers moved in to separate the fighters. Part of the crowd jeered while the rest clapped and consulted their programs.

"Who's next?" A woman in a sparkly dress asked the bald man at her side.

Kaya's heart thumped, but as much as she strained her ears, she couldn't catch the response.

A pair of heavy wooden doors banged open on one side of the arena, and a team of animal handlers hustled the lion out. The crowd booed, hungry for more action. Another crew tended to the injured grizzly, and as they trundled him out, she caught sight of a dozen grim faces peering out from the catacombs. The next fighters, ready for their round?

"Where do they get them all?"

Igor chuckled. "Some volunteer. Others... Let's just say, they are convinced."

She pictured the two thugs slipping Trey a drugged drink, and her blood boiled. To think she'd rescued him from the pits only to have him end up there anyway. Voluntarily, to save her sister and herself.

God, the irony.

A spark escaped her lips, and she nearly jumped back in surprise. Igor had turned away, so she tried it again. Collecting all the threads of her anger on a single breath, she puffed.

A six-inch flame burst out of her mouth. One she barely smothered before Igor turned back, wrinkling his nose. "Is someone smoking in here?"

"Are you nuts?" Karen whispered, grabbing her elbow.

Kaya paled a little. She'd never produced that much fire in her life. Her mind spun with wild ideas through the next three fights.

Then the announcer boomed, "Ladies and gentlemen, Scarlet Palace is proud to present the greatest fighter of them all."

Eager faces peered into the arena as a spotlight darted from archway to archway, teasing them in a guessing game. Which gate might the next fighter emerge from?

"Undefeated in a hundred and thirty fights..."

Kaya stared. Undefeated in *how* many fights?

"Unintimidated, unbeaten, unassailable!"

The crowd hooted in glee.

"The one, the only..."

The whole place hushed for an instant, then went wild when the announcer finally thundered the name. "Kyrill!"

Kaya watched as a bare-chested giant strode into the arena and raised his sword.

A sword? She stared at Karen. What the...?

Kyrill made a slow lap of the arena, acknowledging the crowd as they broke into a frenzy of foot-stomping cheers.

"Ky-rill! Ky-rill! Ky-rill!"

Even from twenty rows up, Kaya could feel the ground shake.

A time machine couldn't have spit out a truer image of a mighty gladiator. Built like an ox and oiled like an oversize engine block, the man strode forward on thickly muscled legs. His face was hidden behind a steel mask, and a blue belt flashed at his waist. One hand gripped the pommel of his sword, while the other brandished a shield so thick, it could serve as a battering ram. With the ornate helmet rising on his head, he had to duck to clear the eight-foot doors of the arena.

Kaya gaped. "A gladiator?"

"The Thracian!" a spectator called, pointing to a page in the program that illustrated various gladiator types.

Women squealed. Men murmured statistics. And an aging shifter sitting not too far from Kaya's seat — a hedgehog shifter, judging by his stature and scent — shook his head.

"I'd hate to be the poor slob who has to fight him tonight."

Right on cue, the announcer launched into a second introduction. "And now, Scarlet Palace introduces Kyrill's opponent."

The crowd whistled and clapped. Some even laughed.

"Our latest and greatest arrival in the pits..."

Across the arena, Kaya spotted Roric leaning forward in another VIP lounge.

"He's mean, he's lean, he's raring for a fight!" the announcer gushed.

Igor smiled smugly and glanced Kaya's way.

"The meanest, wildest wolf in the West..."

Kaya threaded her fingers together and held her breath.

"Black Fang!" the announcer screamed.

The crowd went wild, and Kaya jumped to her feet, shaking, watching the sleekest, darkest wolf she'd ever seen step into the ring.

Chapter Twelve

Trey ground his teeth, watching his opponent strut his stuff.

"Shift." A big, burly guy behind the doors had snapped his fingers at him a second before another yelled, "Showtime!" and threw open the gate.

The place stank of beer, piss, and blood, which only got worse the second he slipped into wolf form. The change came easily, as easy as pulling a cape off or spinning around. He'd barely kept his wolf in check all night, waiting for this moment to come.

His moment to fight for all their lives.

"And stay shifted, you hear?" the handler shouted as Trey took his first steps into the arena.

"Good luck, sucker," an arrogant lion, the victor of the previous fight, muttered as he exited the ring. Then the doors slammed shut behind Trey, and the crowd leaned forward, cheering for blood.

He looked up, trying to locate Kaya, but all he found was the ugly mug of a gargoyle staring down at him from the upper edge of the arena. The place was ringed with statues, and there was no telling which might creak to life to stab him in the back.

The gargoyle cracked an eye open and chuckled, sending a puff of garlicky breath Trey's way. "Prepare to die."

Trey grimaced and stepped farther into the ring. One thing at a time, right? One thing at a time.

Locating Kaya, much as he'd like to fill his tanks on those deep, shining eyes, wasn't important right now. He had to focus on his opponent and take it one step at a time.

Which meant keeping his cool and playing it safe, because the only thing he had to prove tonight was that he could survive. More than survive — he had to win.

He narrowed his gaze on the gladiator, letting the edges of the scene fade away until his whole world tunneled down to that man. He started at the wide, sandaled feet and let his eyes roam past thick thighs to a goofy loincloth thing. Above that was a boxy set of abs and a football field of a chest. Well, what he could make of it behind that blue shield and the glinting edge of the sword. The man wore a steel mask and a Roman centurion helmet.

Christ, did this guy walk right out of the pages of a history book?

The giant smirked, looking down at Trey — or rather, Trey in wolf form. Hell, he would look down even if Trey had remained in human shape, because Kyrill was literally a giant. Not a shifter, just a bigass motherfucker who healed as fast as any shifter. Trey had seen the man carve a knife into his own palm earlier to test the edge of his sword, and the skin had closed up almost instantly.

Great. Just great. A fully armed, self-healing gladiator. Why couldn't he have drawn that slow-witted moose shifter he'd passed on the way in?

A glance up at the cheering arena told him why. Somewhere up there was Igor with two female dragons who faced a fate worse than death if Trey didn't come through.

The gladiator twisted his sword, showing off the glinting blade.

Trey circled right, growling.

"Let the fight begin!" the announcer shouted, and the crowd cheered.

The gladiator stood still, waiting.

Yeah, well. Trey could wait, too. He paced half a lap, then paced back, testing the sand, checking the exits. All of them were locked and glowing with dozens of pairs of interested eyes of whatever backstage crew worked this crazy joint. He wondered who they might be. Shifting rattlesnakes? Wereturkeys, maybe? He'd seen more shifter species on the way through the catacombs than he had in his entire life.

But all he really wanted was to see Kaya one more time. Damn it, he wanted to see her lots more times.

The gladiator rattled the edge of his shield with his sword. "Here, doggie, doggie. Come and get it."

You come and get it, asshole, Trey snarled back.

The gladiator grinned — Trey could just make out the curve of the mouth behind that expressionless mask — and stepped forward, swinging his sword in a figure eight.

"Here, doggie, doggie."

Trey bared his teeth, trying to concentrate. The giant's arm span was so wide, it was hard to keep track of the swinging sword and the outstretched shield at the same time. Which, he supposed, was the point.

Growling, he held his ground. The closer the giant came, the less his peripheral vision could catch. Trey focused on his opponent's shoulders, the point where motion would be triggered.

"Here, doggie, dog—"

The gladiator feinted with the sword then swung his shield like a battering ram. *Whoosh!* The shield sliced the air half an inch from Trey's nose. He leaped backward then dove left, because the sword followed up, cutting through thin air.

The crowd erupted into cheers, and hundreds of feet stomped the floor in unison, calling one name.

"Ky-rill! Ky-rill!"

"Trey!"

His head snapped around, because even in that chaos, he heard Kaya's voice. Maybe he heard it in his mind, where the sound echoed around and around.

As the gladiator advanced, Trey studied him. One arm was protected with a leather gauntlet, but the other was bare. That was the weak point he would have to aim for. That and the guy's unprotected stomach and back, but to get in that close... How the hell would he ever pull that off?

The gladiator tried the same trick. Wide open arms, swinging weapons, taunting calls. A distant corner of Trey's mind registered the fact that the gladiator was a lefty, and tucked that tidbit away. The gladiator faked with the sword, smashed with the shield, and—

Trey timed his jump perfectly, clawing the man's bare arm before jumping clear.

The gladiator roared, more in anger than in pain, and Trey figured that was the easiest blow he would land tonight.

Furious eyes shone from behind the mask.

They circled each other, ignoring the crowd's cheers. The gladiator sliced the air with his sword and stepped forward again. *This time, you die.*

Trey waited in a crouch. The gladiator only had so many moves, he figured, and sooner or later—

The giant came running at him, waving the sword. Same old move, right? Trey leaned left. Too late, he caught the gladiator's shoulders drop. The shield went down, the sword came up, and—

Trey staggered away as a searing line of heat cut into his brow. Something sticky dripped down his ear as he shook his head and rallied.

Blood. He licked his lips and snarled.

A line of ivory curled upward behind the gladiator's mask.

Trey trotted around the ring, trying to reach the giant's unprotected back, but it was no use. The gladiator knew the space well and was prepared for every trick in the book. A book Trey didn't have, because all the fights he'd ever fought were savage wolf encounters that pitted teeth against teeth, and cunning against cunning. This time, he was up against steel and oak.

The gladiator dipped his sword, pointed at Trey, and advanced again. Trey let him come, looking for his chance. If he could catch the giant at exactly the right moment—

The gladiator led with the shield again, crashing it down in a sweeping blow. Trey figured he was prepared, but this time, his foe backhanded the shield. That sent Trey tumbling with a hard blow to the ribs. The gladiator followed up with ungodly speed that belied his bulk, swinging the sword. Trey rolled away a hair ahead of the whistling edge of the blade.

The crowd hooted and cheered. Trey roared into a coun-terattack, jumping onto the gladiator's back and burying his teeth in a shoulder. The wrong shoulder, as it turned out, because that one was armored in layers of leather. He barely drew blood even with his teeth gums-deep.

The gladiator inhaled so hard, Trey could feel his body lift. He clawed at the man's exposed back, but it was no use. Spin-ning, the gladiator heaved Trey off. He went flying into the air and landed with a hard thunk against one of the arched stone entrances. Trey lay there, stunned, until the stars twinkling around his head cleared and—

Shit! He leaped away, a whisker ahead of the slicing blade. The sword clattered off stone with an angry cling.

Then the gladiator backhanded Trey with his shield was in his right. The hard metal edge struck Trey in the ribs, knocking all the air out of him as he rolled away. And rolled and rolled, because it was all his mind could figure to do. Get away. Just get away.

Trey!

Dimly, he wondered if hearing Kaya in his mind was good or bad news. Good, because it meant she was near. Bad, because what if it was the last time?

Trey rolled until he came belly-up against the base of a column built into the perimeter wall and scrambled awkwardly to his feet. The gladiator charged in, following every sliver of an advantage in one long barrage of blows. Trey barely ducked past the crashing edge of the shield and under the gladiator's arm.

He ran to the other side of the arena and stood there, aching, panting, and wondering how he was ever going to win this fight. The gladiator turned and came at him, eager to splay wolf innards all over the ring.

Trey was eager to finish the fight, too, but not like that. It couldn't end like that. He shook his pelt so hard, his teeth rattled as he tried to clear his mind.

Trey, Kaya called. It was a sad, desperate whisper now, like she didn't believe he could pull off a win.

"Get him!" a spectator cried, egging the gladiator on.

God, his ribs hurt.

"Finish him!" a voice that sounded a hell of a lot like Roric's hooted from above.

Blood from a gash he couldn't pick out from all of the others dripped over his brow, stinging his eye.

"Ky-rill! Ky-rill!"

The arena was roaring, but all Trey heard was a distant murmur. His back leg buckled under his body, and he winced.

Trey! No, Trey...

He blinked at his own front feet. Four of them, because he was seeing double now.

Trey! Kaya shouted in a whole new tone. *Get up! Get up now!*

Didn't she know how tired he was? Didn't she know how much it hurt?

You can do it!

He'd never heard her sounding that fierce. That sure.

Get to your goddamn feet, wolf!

The order startled him onto his feet, snarling. Like hell, he would let her down. Like hell, he would lose this fight.

Trey lowered his head as the gladiator rushed in. He held his breath and told his aching ribs to shut up and let him concentrate for a change. Squinting, he shoved everything out of his vision except for one narrow tunnel. Then he counted hundredths of a second, because his timing had to be that good.

Make that, perfect. It had to be perfect.

The gladiator led with the shield as he had every time, and Trey ducked, waiting for his chance. There would be a tiny instant between the shield swinging wide and the upraised sword slicing down.

There! Trey sprang at the gladiator's chest, flattening his ears to slip through the tiny gap that appeared. Like an opening in time, almost, because suddenly, it felt as if time stretched. He could feel the blood rush in his own veins and the gladiator's gasp of surprise, drawn out over several slow heartbeats. Trey dove close — too close for the shield or sword — and every move ticked by in super slow motion. Baring his teeth, he reached for the gladiator's neck. He reached and reached, straining through every millimeter separating him from his foe.

The taste of leather filled his mouth, and he ripped the gladiator's neck guard off the helmet. The pommel of the sword bashed him in the ribs at exactly the same time. Sparks ignited, filling his vision, but that didn't matter any more. The only thing that mattered was the sweaty sheen of the gladiator's exposed neck. Trey clawed the man's chest, ignoring the pommel hammering at this side. The gladiator was making a desperate last stand.

Well, Trey was too. He closed his eyes and dug his jaws into yielding flesh. Warm, sweet blood flooded his mouth, and the world went off-kilter as the gladiator tipped backward, trying to shake him off.

The pounding continued at his side, like a determined visitor at the door to his mind. *Aren't you dead yet?* The knock asked. *Aren't you ready to give in?*

He clamped his jaws tighter and vowed never to let go, no matter what happened. It didn't matter if the gladiator battered him to death, as long as Kaya went free.

Pain threatened to take over, so he put up a mental wall made of a thousand visions of Kaya. Her auburn hair, spread across a pillow. Her flaring cheeks, that time out in the desert when she insisted the car was hers. Her fingers, running over his back...

If he was going to die, he would die with images like that, dammit.

Everything went dim and so hollowly quiet, he didn't know where he was any more. Only that whoever it was under his body had gone very, very still. The roaring in his ears sped up, like a freight train drawing nearer as it screamed down the tracks. Full steam ahead at him, maybe?

He flopped sideways, just in case. Rolling weakly to his side, he tried to coordinate his legs. Somehow, it felt awfully important to get to his feet.

Come on, Trey, you can do it!

Well, if Kaya thought it was important, he might as well try, even if he couldn't see straight.

To win the fight, you have to be on your feet. Get up! It doesn't count unless you're up.

Her voice turned to a yelp of pain, setting off a thousand inner alarms. Reaching into Kaya's thoughts, he felt the sharp dig of Igor's fingernails in her arm, trying to cut her off.

"Shut up!" Igor hissed at Kaya. Trey heard it, clear as a bell.

He heaved a huge breath and jumped to his feet. Then he shook his body, blinking away the sting in his eyes. He peered desperately into the spotlights above until the announcer roared, "The winner! Black Fang wins!"

The crowd exploded into deafening cheers. Trey went limp, crashing sideways onto the sand. But it didn't matter any more because he'd won. The gladiator was wheezing somewhere nearby, not quite dead but defeated all the same.

You did it! Kaya cheered.

He closed his eyes and grinned, because he could feel her smiling at him. He even cracked an eye open, hoping for a glimpse of her face.

Something cackled right over his body, and his blood ran cold, because Kaya didn't cackle. He forced a second eye open and tried to focus on whatever it was.

He gasped, because Kaya didn't have a hooked nose and huge, gaping teeth.

Gargoyles did.

"Prepare to die," snarled the gargoyle hovering ten feet above his body as it dove in.

Chapter Thirteen

Kaya screamed, watching it all unfold. She played everything back a few seconds in her mind, trying to understand.

There was Trey, struggling to his feet, claiming his victory.

She let time tick forward in her mind, then paused it again. There was Trey, collapsing to the ground as the announcer declared him the victor.

And there was the gargoyle, unfolding itself from a marble column.

Her jaw dropped, as the beast extended its claws and moved in. Her ear twitched, picking up Igor's cackle of triumph.

She swiveled her head to the vampire at her side and caught him signaling a second gargoyle off its perch.

Blood roared in her veins as she jumped to her feet.

Karen jumped at the vampire and pummeled him with both fists. "You cheater! You swindler! You piece of shit!"

Kaya stared. Trey had won by the skin of his teeth, fair and square. And now this?

Rage billowed inside her like an out of control wave, and she screamed. "No!"

A six-foot flame erupted from her mouth, and somebody screamed.

"Fire! Fire!"

She shook her head furiously, releasing another whoosh of fire.

"Holy shit," Karen muttered, staring at the dragon muzzle extending from Kaya's face. Then she grinned. "Go, Kaya! Go!"

Kaya barely registered the wings tearing through her shirt or the leathery skin sliding over her like a suit of armor. She

95

barely felt her tail extend as she climbed to the railing of the VIP booth and leaped.

Stale arena air whooshed under her wings as she swooped down toward the ring, intent on the gargoyle diving for Trey.

Never, ever in her life had she managed more than a few sparks, but she was gushing fire now. And, hell — it felt good. Emboldening. Powerful. She spurted another long flame as she folded her wings and dove, searing everything in sight. Including the gargoyle, who turned with a look of horror before spinning sideways, trying to get away.

Whoosh! Another long exhale, and the gargoyle became a flying fireball, gliding through the air.

Kaya snapped her head up and flicked her tail just in time to avoid dive-bombing Trey, who was blinking in confusion on the sand.

Hang on, she urged him. *Hang on!*

She pulled the tightest left-curve of her life and roared at a second gargoyle, who scrambled to fly away. He rose and rose, then dropped into a defensive spiral.

The little sucker thought he could crank a tighter turn than she could, huh? When he pulled out of his dive an inch above the ground, she rolled right after him, sending up little puffs of sand with the tips of her wings. She'd show the bastard...

When she roared, flames folded around the gargoyle and sent him plummeting to the ground.

She whipped her tail and looked around. Two down. How many more to go?

Gargoyles buzzed around her like hornets. The crowd was in chaos, running for the exits.

"Fire! Fire!"

"Oh my God, an electrical fire!" a woman shrieked, pointing at the overhead spotlights.

Electrical fire, my ass. Kaya shot a long, crackling flame toward the witches' control booth above the arena. Three wrinkled faces froze in shock, then dove out of sight.

Third-rate witches, she sniffed and twisted back toward the ring.

Humans stampeded the exits while the shifters in the audience watched Kaya zip by, their mouths agape. All but a single hedgehog shifter who cheered her on.

Kaya nearly cheered, too. She'd never felt so alive. And she'd never felt so tuned in to centuries of dragondom, whose ghosts seemed to peer over her shoulder and applaud. She could do it! She could breathe fire!

It was just like her grandfather said, a long time ago. She could hear his scratchy old voice in her ears.

Fire isn't kindled by greed or desire. Fire is kindled by love, and if you truly believe. . .

She looked at Trey, sprawled on the ground. Her blood seemed to thicken just looking at him, and her soul started to sing. Yes, she could believe. She believed in him — and in the rock-solid certainty that he was the one. Her destined mate.

She glided on that realization for another split second before snapping back to full alert. Three gargoyles zipped toward her in V formation, and she peeled away to the right. First, she rolled, then banked and climbed higher and higher. Finally, she pulled a classic Immelmann turn and swept out of the way. She pulled every dogfighting maneuver her grandfather had taught her, plus a few she invented on the fly. Then she dug the tip of one wing against a pocket of warm air and spun around, catching two of the three gargoyles unprepared. The flame licked her lips as she spat it out. Gargoyles screamed, catching fire. One quick wing-over brought the third gargoyle into her sights, and—

Whoosh! A huge, orange flame reached out and dashed him to the ground.

She bellowed in triumph, sending fire upward like a fountain of reds, oranges, and yellows. Then she looked around. The remaining gargoyles fled back to their perches and turned back to stone. A pumping disco beat filled the air in some DJ's belated attempt to bring normalcy to the scene. Roric, the Westend alpha, popped his head up from where he'd taken shelter under a chair.

Karen plucked Igor's arm off her sleeve and grinned. "*Hasta luego*, asshole." She dusted off her hands and headed for the

97

stairs.

Kaya wrapped her wings around her body, executed a quick three-sixty turn to make sure the danger had passed, and landed at Trey's side.

Hey, she called into his mind, keeping a wary eye on the nearest doors. *Are you okay?*

The answer took so long coming, she could have screamed. Then a weak murmur reached her ears, and Trey rolled to his stomach, panting.

Fine, a pained voice sounded in her head. *Perfect. Great.* He groaned and creaked to his feet.

The gladiator groaned, too, lying nearby in a pool of blood. She could hardly believe he was still alive. Should she finish him off? Give him a second chance?

She bared her teeth, and the gladiator dropped to the ground, playing possum.

Kaya turned to the nearest exit and bellowed in her best dragon voice — a throaty contralto, like that of an opera diva who smoked too many cigars.

"Open the door!"

Silence was the only reply, so she followed up with a fireball that split around the bars and reunited to flood the tunnel beyond.

Out of the corner of one eye, she saw Karen jump from the bottommost level of seats and land cleanly in the sand.

"I'll get your wolf. You get the door," her sister called.

My wolf, Kaya's dragon hummed inside before bellowing again. "Open the door or I'll burn the place down!"

"Coming! Coming!" a timid voice squeaked.

A second later, the gate creaked on its hinges, and four hasty feet scurried away.

Kaya took a cautious step into the dark tunnel. First, she sent a puff of smoke ahead like a scout, then motioned back to her sister, who propped Trey up.

"Let's get out of this joint."

"Yes," Karen replied, pure relief in her voice. "Let's."

Epilogue

Eight hours later...

Trey leaned against the torn headrest of the Jaguar's passenger seat, closed his eyes, and let the sun warm his face. Kaya was driving, and he was way over in the front seat, practically straddling the gear stick — as close as possible to Kaya, which was the main thing. He stroked the back of her neck gently, making her hum as she drove.

"How are you doing?" She put a hand on his thigh.

A little zing went through him, sending excitement and joy on separate paths to the furthest reaches of his body until they reunited somewhere in his chest, wrapped around each other, and glowed for a while.

"Good." He closed his hand over hers. "Really, really good."

He hadn't felt so good in ages. Never mind that his leg still ached and his ribs throbbed. The only thing that mattered was her. Him. *Them.*

The tires hummed over the road, the wind combed his hair, and he laughed.

Kaya turned her head. "What?"

He shook his head. "A couple of days ago, it was so cool to see the Vegas skyline rise on the horizon." He glanced in the sideview mirror. "Now, it feels good to see it disappear."

"Amen. I won't be going back there in a hurry, that's for sure." Kaya's brow wrinkled as she said it, and he knew she was thinking of her sister.

"You sure you're okay with leaving Karen back there?"

Kaya glanced over her shoulder and shook her head as if the gas station twenty miles back was still in sight. "She insisted, so. . ."

That was the crazy thing. Karen had spent the first ten miles of the drive north sitting quietly in the back seat. Too quiet, almost. When they'd stopped at a gas station a little while later, she'd hopped out of the car, stared at the horizon, and finally announced that she had to go back to Vegas.

"You what?" Kaya had screeched.

Trey shook his head, just thinking about it.

Karen had looked at her feet. "Look, I'm grateful you got me away from the vampires, but. . ."

"But what?"

"It's hard to explain. . ." Karen went on.

Kaya stuck her hands on her hips. "We just busted our asses to get you out of there. You could have died. *Trey* could have died." She glowered at her sister and spoke in a growly voice a lot like her dragon's. "You sure as hell better explain."

Karen had shot Trey an uncertain look, then dragged Kaya out of earshot and proceeded to wave her arms, flick her fingers, and explain.

Trey didn't know what she was on about, but in the end, Kaya hadn't pushed her, so he hadn't either.

"Just swear you'll stay away from the slot machines," Kaya had finally said, catching Karen in a huge hug.

"I swear," Karen promised, her voice muffled by her sister's shoulder.

Now, Trey looked in the mirror and squeezed Kaya's hand. "You think she'll be okay?"

"She'd better be okay," Kaya said, more in a sigh than a growl.

He sure hoped so. He'd had enough of Vegas for a lifetime.

And so there they were, just the two of them, heading north in a 1962 Jag.

A sign for Reno flashed by. "You tempted?" Kaya crooked an eyebrow at him.

He snorted. "Not in the least."

100

"Really? The way you played in Vegas, you could easily pick up a couple of thousand bucks."

"And more trouble." He shook his head then pulled her knuckles in for a kiss. "Got all the winnings I need right here."

She smiled her movie-star smile. "You only won one thing."

"The best one," he said, and he meant it. A sign for a rest stop blurred by, and he pointed. "Pull over."

She looked around. "But we already filled the tank..."

"Just pull over."

She put on the blinker, took the off-ramp, and headed for the gas station.

"Around the back," he murmured.

She drove into the curtain of shade behind the building, shut off the engine, and turned to face him. "What do—"

He cut her off with a kiss and pulled her into his lap. Not an easy operation in the tight front seat of the roadster, but a second later, he had her nestled perfectly against his body. Too perfectly, because his wolf was getting bad ideas again.

Good ideas, the wolf growled. *Like marking. Mating. Making her ours for good.*

"Soon," he whispered.

"Soon, what?" She kissed his brow and snuggled closer, straddling him.

He chuckled. "Pretty soon, this wolf isn't going to be able to wait any more."

"Oh, yes?" she teased. "Wait for what?" She ran a finger down his stomach and played with the button of his jeans.

He kissed her neck... Licked the spot he already had scoped out as the perfect place... Nibbled it a little, then whispered against her skin.

"To make you mine."

She tipped his head up and looked deep into his eyes. "I'm already yours."

As if his cock wasn't already straining at the seams of his jeans.

"All the way, mine," he said, nibbling again. "Forever."

101

"Now let me see..." She worked her hands over his shoulders and behind his back, gently massaging the sore spots. "You bite me..."

"Mm-hmm." He nodded, fluttering kisses over her throat. God, her skin was soft.

"...just deep enough to draw a little blood and make us mates..."

He traced the sinews of her neck with his nose. Damn, did she smell good.

"...and what exactly is in it for me?"

She was teasing, but he still gulped. What exactly was in it for her? She would be stuck with him forever. A bruised-up shifter who was good at cards and rustling cattle, with vague plans for a place of his own someday. Okay, not such vague plans, but without the cash to buy the land he needed. Crap, what did mating really get her?

"...other than my favorite wolf, I mean," she went on.

His wolf wagged its tail.

"And other than fabulous sex." She tightened her legs around his hips.

Now that she put it that way...

"Other than a guy who makes me feel like I'm the greatest reward..."

He worked his kisses up to her jawline. "You are the greatest reward."

"Other than the perfect mate for me and the life I always wanted, working a small ranch in Wyoming," she concluded, tipping her forehead to his. "Other than all that, what exactly is in it for me?"

"Well..." His tongue flopped a little, because his soul was still bouncing around in a happy dance, and he couldn't quite gather his thoughts. "We still need to figure out a way to get that ranch in Wyoming. We lost the cash, you know."

The sign for Reno flashed in his mind. He hated the idea, but...

"Forget it." When she cupped his cheek, her face glowed, like that was all she really needed. "The main thing is, we have each other."

He was just getting ready to dive into those luscious lips when she broke into a huge grin. "And hey, we have the car."

He laughed. "You sure do like this car."

"I do." She leaned back, twisting in his lap. "You want to know why?"

He tugged her closer, not ready to give up the contact just yet, but she wiggled away and fumbled with something in the glove compartment.

"Um, because it was your grandfather's car and he left it to you?"

She faced him again, holding a manila envelope up like a lottery ticket. "Want to know what else he left me?"

Trey pursed his lips, wondering what was in there. Season tickets to the local college games? A cryptic sketch marking the way to an old, exhausted mine? Love letters to her grandmother?

She pulled a sheaf of papers out and unfolded them. Long, thick papers with swirly script at the top and a big red seal on the bottom. He squinted and read the hand-printed text on the dry parchment.

Land deed?

She nodded. "The deed to a property my granddad's uncle owned. Three thousand acres, backing right up to the Wind River Range. It hasn't been worked in generations." She raised an eyebrow as if in challenge.

He took the paper out of her hand and stared.

"He left it to you?"

"He left it to me. Well, to Karen, too."

His heart started thumping a little harder. "And you were planning to...?"

"To start up a ranch there once I had a business partner to run it with. And since Karen isn't interested..."

Trey caught both her hands in his and stared into her eyes. His breath caught, and he didn't dare reply.

"There's a little log cabin next to a mountain stream..." she went on.

The heavy parchment of the deed and the dreamy tone in her voice had his imagination galloping away. He knew enough about ranching to get started, and his cousin could help him fill in the gaps. He and Kaya could hole up there over the coming winter and figure out their priorities. He had some savings, which would be a start. Come spring, the two of them could get to work in earnest and...

"So what do you say?" Kaya seemed to be holding her breath, too.

He tried to joke away the lump in his throat. "You think a dragon and a wolf could get along long enough to make it work?"

She grinned. "I think a dragon and a wolf are just what that place needs."

He smiled a moment longer, then crushed her against his chest in a hug so tight, it hurt his ribs. But whatever. The only thing that mattered right now was keeping her close.

"Are you sure?" he murmured, giving her a last chance to rethink.

She laughed. "Never been so sure of anything in my life, wolf." Her lips closed over his in a kiss that quickly jumped the border from warm promise to all-out desire.

"Now then..." She hummed right over his lips. "Let's get back to where we left off."

He ran his hands upward along her ribs. "Where exactly did we leave off?"

It was all mixed up in his mind. One good thing piled on another, like a stack of Christmas presents too high to fit under the tree.

She tipped her head to the side in open invitation. "I vaguely remember something about a mating bite..."

His wolf growled inside as his canines slowly extended.

"Here? Now?"

She popped the top button of his jeans and shimmied out of her shorts. "Maybe I like to live dangerously."

He snorted. He'd had enough living dangerously for a while, but the moment her hand wiggled inside his boxers... Well, why the hell not?

They moved in tandem to work his jeans far enough down to free his shaft, and then she slowly settled over him, one hot, tight inch at a time.

His head thunked back on the headrest as he gave in to the heat zipping through his veins.

"Trey..." she sighed, starting to rock.

He gripped her hips and rocked back, quickly losing hold of the last conscious thought flitting through his mind before lust and instinct took over completely.

He was leaving Vegas with a dragon, a vintage Jaguar, and a bright future. Why was he not surprised?

Sneak Peek: Gambling on Her Bear

Diamond thief falls for burly bear security chief in Vegas. What could possibly go wrong?

Dragon shifter Karen Proulx has a way of tackling big goals head-on. Return to Vegas. Seek revenge on a mortal enemy. Claim a priceless diamond. All very straightforward, right?

And if she hasn't worked out every detail... Well, she'll just call that being flexible. Anyway, she can always wing it if — or more likely, when — things don't go exactly to plan. If only it wasn't for that irresistible bear shifter, getting her all distracted at the worst possible time...

Because of all the things a girl can improvise, love is the trickiest of them all.

Tanner Lloyd is a man on a mission to save his hometown. The key to success will be sticking to the time-honored code of his bear clan: look before you leap, think ahead, and never, ever diverge from your plan.

But along comes Karen, a band of blood-sucking vampires, and a heist that rapidly spins out of control. Before he knows it, he's risking everything for a beautiful stranger and gambling on love, the most unpredictable force of all.

Books by Anna Lowe

Shifters in Vegas

Paranormal romance with a zany twist

Gambling on Trouble

Gambling on Her Dragon

Gambling on Her Bear

Aloha Shifters - Jewels of the Heart

Lure of the Dragon (Book 1)

Lure of the Wolf (Book 2)

Lure of the Bear (Book 3)

Lure of the Tiger (Book 4)

Love of the Dragon (Book 5)

Lure of the Fox (Book 6)

Aloha Shifters - Pearls of Desire

Rebel Dragon (Book 1)

Rebel Bear (Book 2)

Rebel Lion (Book 3)

Rebel Wolf (Book 4)

Rebel Heart (A prequel to Book 5)

Rebel Alpha (Book 5)

Fire Maidens - Billionaires & Bodyguards

Fire Maidens: Paris (Book 1)

Fire Maidens: London (Book 2)

Fire Maidens: Rome (Book 3)

Fire Maidens: Portugal (Book 4)

Fire Maidens: Ireland (Book 5)

Fire Maidens: Scotland (Book 6)

Fire Maidens: Venice (Book 7)

Fire Maidens: Greece (Book 8)

Fire Maidens: Switzerland (Book 9)

The Wolves of Twin Moon Ranch

Desert Hunt (the Prequel)

Desert Moon (Book 1)

Desert Blood (Book 2)

Desert Fate (Book 3)

Desert Heart (Book 4)

Desert Rose (Book 5)

Desert Roots (Book 6)

Desert Yule (a short story)

Desert Wolf: Complete Collection (Four short stories)

Sasquatch Surprise (a Twin Moon spin-off story)

Blue Moon Saloon

Perfection (a short story prequel)

Damnation (Book 1)

Temptation (Book 2)

Redemption (Book 3)

Salvation (Book 4)

Deception (Book 5)

Celebration (a holiday treat)

Serendipity Adventure Romance

Off the Charts

Uncharted

Entangled

Windswept

Adrift

Travel Romance

Veiled Fantasies

Island Fantasies

www.annalowebooks.com

About the Author

USA Today and Amazon bestselling author Anna Lowe loves putting the "hero" back into heroine and letting location ignite a passionate romance. She likes a heroine who is independent, intelligent, and imperfect – a woman who is doing just fine on her own. But give the heroine a good man – not to mention a chance to overcome her own inhibitions – and she'll never turn down the chance for adventure, nor shy away from danger.

Anna loves dogs, sports, and travel – and letting those inspire her fiction. On any given weekend, you might find her hiking in the mountains or hunched over her laptop, working on her latest story. Either way, the day will end with a chunk of dark chocolate and a good read.

Visit AnnaLoweBooks.com

Printed in Great Britain
by Amazon